"How Much Longer Are You Going to Keep Me Dangling?"

"Days, weeks . . . forever, maybe," she retaliated daringly.

"I'll give you time . . . for now. I've never waited for a woman in my life."

Zackery's stark statement triggered an equal honesty in her. "I don't sleep around. I never have and I never will. I also don't make commitments. I walk alone, I live alone and every once in a while I take someone into my life." She paused. "But only on my terms. You're different. You have been from the first. . . ."

SARA CHANCE

is a "wife, mother, author in that order," who currently resides in Florida with her husband. With the ocean minutes from her front door, Ms. Chance enjoys both swimming and boating.

Dear Reader:

SILHOUETTE DESIRE is an exciting new line of contemporary romances from Silhouette Books. During the past year, many Silhouette readers have written in telling us what other types of stories they'd like to read from Silhouette, and we've kept these comments and suggestions in mind in developing SILHOUETTE DESIRE.

DESIREs feature all of the elements you like to see in a romance, plus a more sensual, provocative story. So if you want to experience all the excitement, passion and joy of falling in love, then SILHOUETTE DESIRE is for you.

Karen Solem
Editor-in-Chief
Silhouette Books

SARA CHANCE
This Wildfire Magic

Silhouette Desire

Published by Silhouette Books New York

America's Publisher of Contemporary Romance

Other Silhouette Books by Sara Chance

Her Golden Eyes
Home at Last

 SILHOUETTE BOOKS, a Division of Simon & Schuster, Inc.
1230 Avenue of the Americas, New York, N.Y. 10020

Copyright © 1983 by Sydney Ann Clary

Distributed by Pocket Books

ISBN: 0-671-49860-6

First Silhouette Books printing December, 1983

10 9 8 7 6 5 4 3 2 1

America's Publisher of Contemporary Romance

Printed in the U.S.A.

Passion is the fire of love
Sensuality is a wild spirit set free
Their mating is potent magic
Its strength endures eternity.

This Wildfire Magic

1

~~~~~~~~~~~~~

A lush green meadow lay bathed in the golden rose haze of the setting sun. The scent of wildflowers drifted with the gentle breeze that teased the leaves of the stately trees surrounding the peaceful glen. A lone figure stood in the ankle-deep grass—a woman, tall, slender, draped in a long emerald nightgown of fluid silk. The delicate folds clung to her form with a lover's embrace as she paused, silhouetted against the slowly darkening evening sky.

Suddenly the crack of a twig crushed underfoot disturbed the eerie waiting silence. The woman stiffened, instantly wary. Her gaze swung to the shadows at the edge of the clearing. A dark form moved out of the trees to step into the light of the meadow. Eyes the color of deep brown velvet looked out of a face tanned gold by the sun. Held by the intensity of the man's stare, the woman barely noticed his muscular frame clothed in a white shirt open at the neck and dark trousers.

Mesmerized by the strange visual hold the alien had on her, she made no effort to flee as the shadowy figure padded slowly toward her. Closer he came, his fathomless eyes keeping her frozen in place, the scent of him wrapped around her, entrapping her senses.

She wanted to run, to flee as fast and as far as she could, but she was powerless to command her limbs to obey.

He reached out his hand, his fingers tracing a tantalizingly gentle pattern across the smoothness of her cheek. At the tenderness of his single gesture, her panic died, replaced by an emptiness, a yearning.

Her gaze locked with his and read the desire mirrored in the inky depths. She swayed toward him, drawn by his need and hers. His lips parted, her breath mingled with his as she felt the warmth of his mouth possess . . .

An insistent burr shattered the dream into tiny fragments. Desiree groaned in protest as she was jerked out of her beautiful fantasy. Opening one eye just enough to sight her alarm clock, she shut it off with a well-practiced slap of her hand. For a moment she lay without moving while her mind made the abrupt switch from sleep to wakefulness. Accustomed to her unusually vivid dreams, Desiree expected her nocturnal images to fade as they usually did, leaving behind only the germ of an idea for a new nightgown design. But not this morning. The dark-eyed male lingered, or rather the compelling memory of his eyes and the feelings they had created did.

Desiree considered this new phenomenon carefully. For years—ever since she had started designing clothes—she had found her dreams populated with shadowy female forms inhabiting different settings. Each vignette had always been simply a background to display some gown or outfit that her imagination had created. When she awoke, she was left with a new idea which she then sketched and perfected.

Yet for some reason, this morning the pattern was different. She did have her design, but she also had a man. That had never happened before.

Where had he come from? she wondered with a kind of uneasy amusement. He looked like no one she knew, that was for sure. Unconsciously, Desiree ran the tip of her tongue over her lips, then shrugged.

"Oh well, I suppose at my age a woman is allowed a fantasy lover or two," she mocked herself lightly.

Sliding out of bed, she reached for her sketching pad and colored pencils that she'd placed on the table the night before. With Laura occupying her guest room, which also doubled as a workroom, Desiree had had to make do with drawing on her lap pad instead of her board. Concentrating on the gown the woman in the dream had worn, Desiree banished her unexpected night visitor to the realms of her memory. Taking care not to awaken her weekend guest, she crept down the hall to her living area. The drapes of the floor-to-ceiling windows were open, framing the slowly lightening sky. Desiree focused on the purple to mauve sunrise, enjoying the peace of her favorite part of the day. Soft fingers of light drifted through the windows, highlighting her pink, silk-clad figure as she stood poised before the glass. A tumbled mass of ash brown curls brushed her shoulders while her unusual

11

deep green eyes shot with sparks of gold drank in the beauty and serenity of the spectacle unfolding before her.

The delicate shadings were reminiscent of her dream, calling to mind a vivid picture of the green nightgown.

"Emerald Enchantment," she whispered softly, testing the easy slip of syllables with her husky, drawling voice. Pleased at the sound, she smiled. The name fitted the gown to perfection. Enchantment, like most of the nightwear she had designed lately, was a provocative statement of a woman's femininity and a tantalizing challenge to a man's instinctive desire for beauty, softness and visual stimulation. Eager to begin her newest sketch, Desiree glided toward the mauve sofa, her bare feet sinking into the lavender gray carpet with each step. She tucked herself into the velvet-covered couch, her slender curves nestling in the overstuffed cushions with an unconscious appreciation of comfort.

Delicate, fine-boned fingers gripped the drawing pencil as she began to translate her mind's creation into the strong, bold strokes so at odds with her quiet, watchful personality. Brilliance, style and her own unique flair for fashion flowed effortlessly onto the sheet as Emerald Enchantment emerged in all its seductive glory. Hours flew by as Desiree lost herself in the world of her imagination.

A deep plunging bodice rippled from a feathery froth of lime maribu shoulder straps to reveal a tantalizing glimpse of the wearer's curves. From the base of the slit, tiny pleats of pin-tucked, light green satin radiated across the waist and hips all the way to the maribu-trimmed, ankle-length hem in a stunning starburst effect which was both slimming and unusual. Over this confection, Desiree fashioned a sheer cape of silk chiffon banded in the same feathers as the gown.

When she had finished, she dropped her pencil in her lap and stared at her drawing. A tiny frown marred the smooth perfection of her honey-toned skin. Something was missing, she decided. Seconds ticked by as she surveyed the clean lines of her rendering. Then she smiled, her face clearing magically.

"A miniature silk orchid," she pronounced with pleased delight. "Right here." She quickly drew the exotic bloom in the base of the plunging neckline, then leaned back once again to study her creation.

"You look like the cat who swallowed the proverbial canary," Laura grumbled groggily as she stumbled into the living room. She flopped limply into a lilac armchair near Desiree. "Don't tell me you have another idea. You've got the most indecently wicked mind I know."

Desiree glanced up, eyeing her former college roommate through half-closed lashes with her usual unblinking stare. "Okay, I won't tell you," she teased, ignoring the last part of her friend's indictment. She was too well accustomed to Laura's caustic manner to be offended.

Laura pushed back her pale gold hair with an irritated gesture. "I swear I don't know how you can get out of bed looking so darned sexy. It's not as if you're gorgeous or anything." She gestured graphically to her own crumpled state before glaring mildly at Desiree's flowing silk gown that hugged her delicately curved figure. Thigh-high slits exposed a glorious length of slender legs while the faintly oriental cut of the bodice revealed a great deal of her velvet-soft breasts.

"That's new, isn't it," Laura commented, an appreciative gleam lighting her hazel eyes.

Desiree nodded, an imp dancing in her unwavering gaze. "And before you start nagging at me to design you one like it, let me tell you right now that I won't," Desiree replied frankly. She chuckled at Laura's disappointed expression.

"Stinker!" her friend shot back before laughing aloud. She glanced down at her own voluptuous figure. "It definitely wouldn't be one of my better ideas if I tried to trick myself out to look like you." She curled her feet up under her and wiggled into a more comfortable position. "I've often wondered how we ever got to be such friends; it's the age-old chalk and cheese routine all over again."

Desiree's assent touched her features with self-mockery. "I know. I'm the tall beanpole to your pocket-sized Venus, the slow, easygoing foil to your supercharged energy, and the plain Jane to your gorgeous blonde."

"Fiddle!" Laura retorted inelegantly, destroying the effect of the expensive finishing-school poise she and Desiree shared. "I'd give my eyeteeth to wake up with that tousled, just-made-love-to look you have. I hate that wavy silver brown hair of yours. It reminds me of a Siamese cat, it's so strokable. I wanted some of my own, but my hairdresser told me it wouldn't work." Admiration and affection colored Laura's half-serious rebuttal. "And five foot ten is not anyone's idea of a beanpole even by your own strange southern logic. As for your so-called laid-back disposition—that's the biggest laugh of the year. You're the *only* person I know who would get up at dawn to draw a nightgown you dreamed up. Speaking of which, how about letting me see this new work of art?"

"I was hoping you'd ask, Miss Hotshot Clothes Buyer from Houston," Desiree retaliated, passing Laura her pad. She slipped smoothly off the couch. "While you're looking, I'll make us some coffee." She smiled at Laura's rapt attention to the drawings filling her book. "It's my new line; I named it Dream Magic. So far I've got three decent gowns." She drifted toward the kitchen, hearing the faint rustle of paper as Laura studied each exotic fantasy. While she prepared the percolator, she visualized the negligees she had fashioned: Sweet Surrender, an image of virginal white and daring sexuality; Savage Seduction, searing scarlet blazing with the enthralling powers of womanhood; and lastly, this morning's effort, Emerald Enchantment.

"Well?" Desiree prompted when she returned to the living room carrying the coffee tray.

Laura looked up, the light of battle sparking in her eyes. All vestiges of sleep and long-time camaraderie were wiped from her expression. She was all business and Desiree noted the change with a carefully concealed sigh. She should have known this would happen. Here it came—another lecture on her ambition, or lack thereof.

"These are great. Where are you sending them?" Laura asked with her usual bluntness.

Desiree took her time answering, busying herself with preparing her coffee before resuming her half-sitting, half-reclining sprawl on the sofa. She took a sip from the fine bone-china cup she held while she studied Laura's determined face. For a moment she wondered why she had given Laura the sketches to look over. Was she secretly hoping Laura would give her the drive she lacked? No, it couldn't be that, she decided. After all, she was very happy as Manuelo's assistant. True, some of his fashions were less dramatic than she herself would have used. But still . . . Unwilling to remember the vague stirrings of restlessness which had been dogging her footsteps the last few months, Desiree returned her attention to the matter at hand.

"I'm not sending them anywhere," she denied finally.

"Why not?" Laura demanded, sitting forward in her seat. Aggression bristled in every line of her diminutive body as she swung her legs to the floor and slapped the pad she held on her knee. "Surely you're not going to tack these fabulous nightgowns on that stupid corkboard of yours for a month and then poke them in your portfolio where they'll never see the light of day again. I won't let you."

Desiree shrugged evasively. "Maybe."

Her seemingly indifferent reply brought a deep frown to her tormentor's expression. Laura glared at her. "Do you realize how few people actually design sleepwear with the class and eye appeal you do? A handful!" she all but shrieked in frustration. "You portray sex, sensuality and seduction in every blasted line and still my grandmother could buy one of these and enjoy wearing it without feeling like some five-dollar tramp on the make."

"What an expression," Desiree teased lightly, blatantly shutting her ears to the tirade she had heard in various forms so often before. Next time, she vowed silently, she'd keep her big mouth shut and her sketches under lock and key.

"Desiree Beaumont, honestly, I could murder you sometimes," Laura exclaimed, the dangerous glint in her eyes more than backing up her declaration. "You're not listening to a word I say."

Desiree shrugged slightly, the movement of her bare shoulders daring the provocative low cut of her bodice to stay in place. "I've heard it all before both from you and my parents. We've known each other since boarding school and, since we're both only a few months short of thirty, I thought you knew me better than anyone. I've never made any secret of my aversion to the success you strive for," she explained patiently, the picture of calm reasonableness.

"Desiree, please think. It's criminal to stay in that job of yours. You're worth ten of that man you fetch and carry for." Laura's voice held a hint of pleading.

"You're being melodramatic, Laura. Most unlike you." Desiree leaned forward, filling the extra cup on the tray and passing it to her friend. "I won't hawk my drawings." Finality was etched in every word of her flat decree.

Laura sipped her coffee in momentary silence, a thoughtful expression dispelling some of her annoyance. "What if I told you I know someone who would jump at the chance to introduce a line like this?"

Intrigued in spite of herself at Laura's confident tone, Desiree halted in her automatic refusal. "Who?" she voiced impulsively, immediately regretting the question when she saw her friend's triumphant smile.

"Zackery Taylor Maxwell. Taylor/Maxwell to be precise," Laura elaborated, naming one of the better-known ready-to-wear houses.

"You're nuts," Desiree observed, surprised by the suggestion of the famous corporation and its equally renowned head. "They have a perfectly good design-er line of their own. What would they want with me? It doesn't fit their image at all."

Laura waved her hand in exasperation. "I can't believe you said that. You know as well as I do anything new and unique is in demand. Have you looked at these sketches of yours—really looked?" Laura demanded incredulously.

"Don't be an idiot. Of course I know what I drew," Desiree returned, a slight edge creeping into her voice. Her lashes raised to impale Laura with a tawny emerald stare of irritation. "You know this is a hobby for me—you've always known it. Why this sudden push to make it something more?"

Laura slid her empty cup and saucer onto the table between them. Her determined eyes clashed with Desiree's. "Because I'm tired of seeing you hide your talent in some misguided attempt to deny your heritage."

Sheer shock held Desiree motionless, suspended in disbelief. "Is that what you think I'm doing?" she questioned finally.

Laura nodded, a faintly puzzled look entering her eyes.

Desiree stared at her friend, unable to comprehend Laura's misjudgment. If there were anyone in her life she would have said knew her, it was Laura. And yet Laura credited her with this juvenile rebellion. It was unthinkable—incredible.

A part of her was hurt, but another part knew she really had no right to be, for as close as the friends were, Desiree rarely discussed her family or her abortive marriage with Laura. Suddenly she felt the need to talk and give voice to the feelings she normally held silent. Swinging her feet to the floor, she sat up, facing Laura.

"I'm not hitting back at my parents or even

Jeremy," she began evenly. "Any bitterness or anger I had for them died years ago. My mother and father are who they are and I'm me. Just as Jeremy chose his own way, I'll make mine—but it won't be in the marketplace. Business, especially big business, worships the gods of power and money. It lures ordinary people like my parents and my ex-husband with golden promises, doling its favors out one by one until its victims are addicted. It teaches its followers to use people, to discount emotion and to ignore integrity. I won't be one of its devotees." She paused, spreading her hands in quiet resignation. "In many ways my marriage, short as it was, showed me a lot about myself."

"What could that power-hungry idiot you married have possibly taught you?" Laura retorted indignantly. "Don't forget I was there when you found out that he'd chosen you because you were your father's only child and heir to the Beaumont Corporation."

Desiree's lips twisted in a rueful smile of acknowledgment. "I'll admit my ego got a little battered." Her smile widened at Laura's quirked eyebrow, expressing her opinion of that understatement. "The thing is, Jeremy showed me a whole new world, a place where I finally felt I belonged. For years I was like a duck in a nest of swans until I recognized my own nature."

"So what's this great gift that louse gave you?" Laura's sharp query carried her long-standing dislike for the man Desiree had once wed.

"He gave me a glimpse of passion and the magic of my senses. True, it was only for a moment, but somehow it righted my life. I quit blaming my parents for their distant caring. With their ambition and drive, there was really no other way for either of them.

Having a child did nothing to change my father into a doting parent nor my corporate lawyer mother into a model of maternal virtue. I don't hold Jeremy guilty either for wanting to achieve success, although I do count him wrong in the way he used me to reach his goal. But even that no longer holds any pain for me. He and my family are happy with his promotion in the agency. Whatever he may be as a man, he is damn good at his work."

"I still don't understand what that has to do with your drawings and your refusal to market them," Laura stated, looking confused. "So Jeremy taught you about sex. So what?"

"Not sex, Laura," Desiree corrected. "He taught me about responding to the world. For the short time I believed Jeremy loved me, I let go my inhibitions. I decorated our apartment with all the colors I'd always longed to have around me; we had satin sheets, velvet cushions, carpets deep enough to wade in. Not a white wall, piece of marble or slick glass in sight. It was glorious, and for the first time in my life I loved where I lived. Coming from that cold mausoleum my family calls home, I was in heaven. I was alive, not just existing." Desiree turned her hands palms up in a gesture of supplication. "So you see, I'm not rebelling against my heritage so much as trying to protect my identity. I don't ever want to become like my parents. That's why I don't want to peddle my designs and it's also why I'm content to fetch and carry, as you call it, for Manuelo."

Desiree noted the compassion and understanding warming Laura's eyes at the end of her explanation. She waited silently, expecting her friend to withdraw her demand that Desiree show her sketches.

"Will you let *me* sell your line for you?"

"You?" Desiree echoed, momentarily at a loss.

Laura nodded. "Yes." It was her turn to plead. "These are just too good to ignore. And frankly, I don't really believe you want to hide them away or you wouldn't have shown them to me in the first place."

"Perhaps," Desiree conceded, weighing the validity of Laura's claim. Maybe she did want to see her fantasy come to life. She knew her recent sketches were the best work she'd ever done. Maybe Laura was right. Maybe they did deserve a chance. Suddenly her restlessness returned, crystalizing into an urge to do something. About to refuse Laura's suggestion, Desiree found her voice disobeying her commands. "I'll give them to you, but only on one condition—I won't haggle over the price. I'll look over the contracts before I sign if the offer is good. I've learned enough about corporate law from listening to my mother to know what I want and what I don't. One thing I don't wish is to be hassled about my work. A nice quick, clean sale or nothing."

Laura's surprise was clear although she was quick to agree to Desiree's stipulation. "Fair enough. What do you say we go out to lunch to celebrate?" she suggested quickly as she rose from her chair, apparently worried that Desiree would change her mind. "Just give me an hour to make myself presentable." She hurried toward her bedroom, the sketch pad tucked protectively under one arm. "Is shopping afterwards okay with you?"

"Fine," Desiree murmured as Laura disappeared down the hall. Realizing what she'd just agreed to, Desiree was surprised to find that she didn't regret her decision. What was wrong with her? Why this sudden desire to change her life? She had her home, her job and the artistic freedom she'd always craved. Even her parents had ceased to nag her about her easygoing lifestyle and her peculiar—to their way of thinking, anyway—interest in clothes designing. What else did she want?

Excitement, a little voice whispered. A piece of her fantasies, a touch of the magic she saw only in her dreams. And she wanted Dream Magic to come to life, she acknowledged with a flash of insight. She wanted to see the flow of her gowns when they draped a human form. With this admission, she knew an intense feeling of relief. An unexpected surge of anticipation flowed through her. Rising, she smiled wryly as she cleared away the coffee tray and headed for her room to get ready.

Filling her tub with bath essence and warm water, Desiree immersed her body in the frothy bubbles. The scented cloud caressed her skin with silken warmth as she gently smoothed the sponge across her shoulders and down her throat to her breasts. Normally it was her custom to linger until the cooling temperature forced her out, but not today.

Restless energy coursed through her, demanding an outlet. Quickly completing her ablutions, she dried her delicately perfumed skin, left the damp towel in the steamy bathroom and returned to her bedroom to survey her closet with dissatisfaction. Not a thing to wear, she observed in silent mockery as she flipped through the elegantly classic garments that comprised her everyday wardrobe. Beige, oyster, white, gray, lavender . . . bare touches of color compared to the vivid rainbow of her exotic sleepwear. Suddenly she disliked the cool, unhurried public image she had so painstakingly built for herself. She glanced around her gloriously colorful bedroom, then back at her quietly reserved closet. The contrast was as striking as the shades and hues which decorated her private life and her fantasies. A flicker of distaste marred her smooth features as she finally chose a sleeveless white shantung sheath and matching jacket. After extracting a lace braslip, garter belt and bikini panties in champagne silk, she quickly slipped into the wisps of undercovering before perching on the end of her rose velvet chaise to put on her stockings. When she finished, she stood and surveyed her image in the mirror for a moment, wondering why she had such a fetish about sexy underclothes and nightgowns. She smiled lazily at the tousled girl staring back at her.

"Maybe I'm just a courtesan at heart," she purred wickedly before reaching for the conventional day dress waiting for her to step into.

"Desiree, are you ready yet?" Laura's voice, muffled by the closed door, drew Desiree's attention.

"Come on in," she invited, casting a quick glance at the clock as she sat down in front of her makeup mirror. She gestured to the chair near her vanity as Laura strolled over. "I only have my face left to do."

Her friend dropped into the tufted chair, crossed her legs and glared mildly at Desiree. "I swear if I sighted you by a telephone pole, you wouldn't have moved four inches in the past hour," she grumbled, eyeing Desiree's movements as she carefully made up. "Don't you ever get an urge to do anything quickly?"

Desiree finished stroking on her bronze-tinted lip color with a practiced hand. "If I do, I stifle it," she replied solemnly, despite the gleam of devilish humor lurking in her odd-colored eyes. "It's bad for the image, you know." She shrugged slightly and then reached for her hairbrush.

"I give up," Laura conceded on a gurgle of laughter. "I should have known better than to tease you. In all the years I've known you, you haven't changed one iota. You're still the most self-sufficient, independent, indolent, brilliant creature I've ever met. I'll bet you were a cat in one of your past lives."

Accustomed to Laura's reincarnation beliefs, Desiree continued to style her hair in its usual braided loop at the base of her neck. "You know I don't look a bit feline," she denied absently as she tucked in an errant silver-brown curl. She blinked her long sable lashes one last time to be sure her mascara was dry.

"Oh no!" Skepticism dripped from Laura's short rebuttal. "Physically you're right, except for your Siamese-cat-colored hair and those greeny gold eyes. But in every other way you're more like a cat than a cat is itself."

Moving with characteristic supple grace, Desiree rose, slipped into her white jacket and collected her handbag. "Let's go," she announced, hoping to end Laura's dissertation before it began.

Laura followed her obediently, but continued her monologue. "Just look at this apartment, for example. Everything in it is soft, comfy and disgustingly restful. Not a jarring note anywhere."

"I know," Desiree replied dampeningly. If she were the cat, Laura without a doubt was a bulldog, she mused perceptively to herself.

"You do just enough to get by, too," she went on undaunted in the face of Desiree's blatant disinterest. "Isn't there anything you want enough to exert yourself?" she demanded, taking two quick steps for every one of Desiree's long, lazy strides.

Desiree carefully locked the outer door before answering. "A bit of peace from the make-over-Desiree lecture number three hundred," she returned half seriously as she moved languidly toward the elevator at the end of the hall.

Laura wrinkled her nose expressively. "I'm not trying to remodel you," she argued, trailing her taller friend into the empty elevator.

Desiree glanced down at Laura's expressive face, making no effort to disguise the irony evident in her own. "Aren't you?" She shook her sleek head gently. "Odd, how mistaken I can be after all these years." The silver doors slid noiselessly open, revealing the modernistic glass and steel lobby of her apartment building. "Maybe I should reconsider letting you have my designs," she murmured as if to herself.

"I surrender," Laura capitulated immediately on the heels of the soft-voiced threat. "I promise I won't mention another word about changing your designs or cats for the rest of my visit."

Desiree smiled complacently, then gestured toward the sunny day awaiting them. "Where would you like to have lunch? The Midnight Sun or the Sun Dial?" she asked, naming two of Atlanta's more famous restaurants in the nearby Peachtree area of the city.

"We had dinner at the Midnight Sun the last time I was here, didn't we?"

Desiree nodded as she pushed open the door and was assailed by the warmth of the late August morning. "Considering how you went into raptures over their fountain atrium, I'm surprised you need to ask."

"I can't help it if I fell in love with that gorgeous

place. All that glass, those colored lights and the open sky above was breathtaking, you can't deny it."

"You still haven't told me where you want to go," Desiree reminded her as a taxi screeched to a halt in front of them in response to her imperious summons.

"The Sun Dial, of course." She grinned, obeying Desiree's prodding from behind to get into the cab.

"Do you know what I'm going to do when you leave Monday?" Desiree demanded in fond exasperation after giving directions to the driver.

Laura shook her head, her blond hair swinging gently about her shoulders. "What?"

"I'm going to take a week's rest to recuperate." She held up one hand. "So far this morning I've had one major career decision before breakfast"—she folded her forefinger to her palm—"had my bath scandalously rushed"—down went another finger—"jumped into my clothes"—three—"been compared to a damn cat"—number four—"and finally been insulted because I'm supposedly slower than molasses in a January snowstorm." She impaled Laura with an unblinking stare, noting the rapid rise and fall of her friend's breathing. "Why are you out of breath?"

"I was running to keep up with you—" Laura clapped her hand to her mouth, her eyes widening comically at the trap laid for her. "You rebel! I swear you're impossible. You look like you're out for a leisurely stroll but I have to skip along beside you just to stay even. Darn you and that long-legged stride of yours." She groaned in defeat, Desiree's old college nickname escaping unconsciously.

"We may look slow down here, Yankee girl, but we're not," she drawled in a purposefully thick southern accent.

An audible choke of amusement drew both women's attention to the front seat. Desiree glanced at Laura, one slender brow arched in humorous inquiry. In her desire to score off her diminutive companion, she had forgotten her captive audience. Laura shrugged, her eyes dancing with suppressed laughter. The cab drew to a stop at their destination just in time.

Desiree paid the fare, managing to retain a solemn expression until the taxi drew away. But it didn't last. One look at Laura's face released the giggles bubbling within her. In seconds both of them were laughing uproariously.

Somehow that incident set the tone for the day. The two women entered the glass-enclosed elevator on the outside of the Peachtree Plaza Hotel, reminiscing about their college days together. The nonstop ten-story ride to the revolving restaurant atop the hotel was punctuated with Desiree's running commentary on her favorite city and Laura's appreciative exclamations. Lunch at the spectacular trilevel restaurant lounge was passed in a pleasant atmosphere of excellent food and plush surroundings, in perfect harmony with the crown jewel of the New South cities, the "Big A."

Afterwards, Desiree led Laura on a shopping expedition through the dramatic Peachtree Center. There, gracefully soaring causeways connecting office towers mingled with shops and restaurants. While contemporary sculptures provided a stimulating visual appeal, splashing fountains and benches set among huge pots of yellow chrysanthemums offered fragrant resting places for weary shoppers.

It was late afternoon by the time they returned to Desiree's apartment.

"Remind me never to accuse you of laziness again." Laura sighed, tiredly brushing a blond tendril of hair back from her sun-flushed face. She surveyed her taller companion's pristine appearance with a marked lack of pleasure. "You look like you just stepped out of a cool shower."

Desiree removed her jacket and tossed it over the back of the living room couch. Kicking off her soft leather heels, she curled into one corner of the sofa, her feet tucked under her. "Shopping was your idea," she pointed out calmly, refusing to apologize for their energetic afternoon.

Laura flicked an expressive hand toward the miniature mountain of packages occupying the opposite end of the couch. "Yes, but only two of those are mine." She tipped her disheveled head to one side, curiosity evident in her expression. "Since when have you taken to wearing vivid colors outside your bedroom?" she queried with her usual lack of subtlety.

Desiree shrugged lightly, unwilling to tell Laura of her sudden dissatisfaction with her wardrobe. "It was just an impulse," she answered evasively. She glanced down at her white outfit. "Maybe I'm just going through early midlife crisis."

Laura's eyebrows climbed dramatically at Desiree's uncharacteristic comment. "You? I don't believe you've gone through a crisis in your entire life. Why, even your breakup with Jeremy was so damn polite and calm, it was unbelievable."

At the mention of her ex-husband, Desiree remembered the sense of betrayal she had felt all those years ago. Polite? Calm? she echoed silently. If only Laura knew how much she had longed to scream out her pain and anger at her own naive stupidity in believing

Jeremy's slick protestations of love. Although now she could recognize the good that had come out of her marriage, she still bore the scars of her education. Forcing back the memories of her youthful mistake, she focused on her guest.

"There wasn't much point in getting upset just because Jeremy turned out to be more interested in partnership in Beaumont Advertising Corporation than he was in me." She met Laura's skeptical look steadily. "There are those who strive to achieve and do, like my father, my mother and Jeremy." She paused, then added, "And you. Then there are people like me who ease through life, choosing the softest path to walk."

Horror clouded Laura's eyes as she leaned forward. "You can't possibly mean any of that, can you? I'm not like your parents or that creep you married, and I know darn well you aren't as lazy as you'd like everyone to believe. Sure, I like success, but I'm not going to live in a cold, barren world filled with things and no people. I'm sure not marrying some poor sucker just to skip a couple of rungs on the success ladder I could easily climb on my own."

"Thanks," Desiree murmured sarcastically at Laura's succinct summation of her marital disaster.

Laura ignored her muttered comment. "You know I've spent most of today feeling guilty about prodding you into giving me those Dream Magic sketches, but not anymore. I'm beginning to think it's the best idea I've ever had. It's high time you made a change in your life. I think this is going to be just the ticket. Maybe if you get out into the world you say you hate so much, you'll see it's no better or worse than any other. Who knows, you might even find yourself a man." She grinned wickedly. "Maybe somebody to light those fires of yours."

Desiree's brow quirked at her blatant challenge. "Just stick to selling my Dream Magic and leave my fires to me," she retorted quellingly. "I wouldn't have a businessman lover on a silver platter."

2

~~~~~~~~~~~~~

Desiree leaned her cheek against the cool glass of the airplane window and peered down at the city below her. Houston, golden buckle of the Sunbelt and undeniably the world's energy capital, lay beneath her in all its sprawling majesty. It was difficult to believe that giving Laura her Dream Magic line to sell had brought her halfway across the country. Her eyes traced the tall, sleek and modern skyscrapers, and she felt a decided sense of unreality. Six weeks ago, she had only known Taylor/Maxwell's by reputation. Now here she was up in the clouds both figuratively and literally because of Taylor/Maxwell's influence in her life.

Casting a quick glance at her watch, Desiree sighed softly, impatient to touch ground once more. The flight from Atlanta had seemed hours longer than it really was, a condition in no way alleviated by the compulsive chatter of the woman sitting next to her.

"I'll bet there's something wrong with the landing gear and they're just not telling us," her companion babbled nervously, darting a look at the illuminated seat belt sign.

"It's only a holding pattern," Desiree soothed quietly, stifling the impulse to ask the woman beside her to hush. She could feel the beginnings of a headache edging around her consciousness and right now all she wanted was a cool, quiet place to lie down. In fact, what she really needed was the peace of her old life, not the pulsating energy of this new venture.

Reviewing the last two hectic weeks, she wondered how she had managed to finish everything in time. From the moment she had hung up from Laura's ecstatic phone call announcing Taylor/Maxwell wanted an exclusive on her every design, she had known there was no turning back. What she hadn't counted on was the speed with which the international firm moved. In just days she had been contacted by the head man's private secretary with detailed instructions concerning her relocation to Houston, flight connections, hotel reservations and legal appointments for the all-important contracts. There had even been an offer to secure more permanent housing, which Desiree had turned down flat. The disembodied, crisp voice droning orders in her ear had seemed to herald the end of an era. She had hung up the phone and glanced around her apartment, suddenly realizing that, for the contract's duration, she would be based in Houston. The irritation at the precise demands of her soon-to-be-boss had mingled with a deep regret over leaving the home she had created for herself. Yet among the myriad feelings that had assailed her, excitement over the changes in her life had remained. She knew she preferred the peace of her more ordered, solitary life on a permanent basis, but she had welcomed the exhilaration of what lay ahead.

"Ladies and gentlemen, we are now making our final approach for Houston Intercontinental Airport. We hope you have enjoyed your flight with us. . . ."

Finally, Desiree offered a silent prayer of thanks on hearing the familiar voice of their first-class stewardess offering the airline's standard farewell speech. Moments later, the big jet touched lightly down on the Texas soil. Desiree found the preferential treatment she had been accorded on her flight was only a prelude to what awaited her within the huge, bustling terminal. She was met by a woman from Taylor/ Maxwell who was about her own age and escorted to a waiting silver limousine which whisked her to her hotel. Her escort stayed just long enough to see her settled in her spacious suite and to remind her of her appointment for ten o'clock the next morning before she departed with a friendly smile of welcome.

Feeling slightly breathless at the consummate skill with which her arrival had been handled, Desiree stood staring blankly at the closed door of her sitting room. All of this just for one little contract? She glanced around the luxuriously appointed salon, feeling more bemused than ever. She had expected a nice room, but nothing like this. The royal blue carpet was a fitting complement to the fluid lines of Louis XIV furniture in the stunningly dramatic blue, white and gold suite. Wide double doors opened to the left, revealing an alabaster, satin-covered bed beneath a stylized canopy of royal blue velvet. A splash of deep yellow on the night table drew Desiree's eyes. Roses?

She crossed the room to remove the tiny florist's card peeking discreetly from the thorny foliage. The delicate scent of the half-open blooms whispered about her as she studied the bold script on the amber square she held.

Welcome to my city. May your dreams here be as beautiful as your designs.

                    Z.T. Maxwell

Desiree tapped the cryptic message against her lips and stared thoughtfully at the fragrant bouquet. What an odd choice of words, she mused. In fact, the whole situation was decidedly unusual. First, the VIP treatment at the airport, the suite, then this. She'd heard of wooing an artist, but surely this was slightly more than that. Vaguely uneasy without knowing why, Desiree tossed the card on the table beside the cut-glass vase. She could feel the headache that had been threatening all day begin to throb in earnest. Pressing her fingers to her temples in a futile attempt to massage away the pain, she silently cursed the unexpected return of her unexplained malady. She hadn't had one in years, not since she had moved out of her parents' home. She knew from painful experience that she'd better take something for it now, otherwise she'd be unable to stave off a migraine attack, guaranteed to lay her low for days. With a grimace of disgust at her own weakness, Desiree used the decorator French phone on the table before her to dial room service.

The pleasantly impersonal voice that answered immediately, as well as the prompt knock on her outer door a few moments after she hung up, was further evidence of the unusual solicitude surrounding her. After swallowing the painkillers she had requested,

Desiree took a quick shower, for once more interested in the oblivion of sleep than what she was going to wear to get there. The dull throb in her head seemed to intensify with every step as she padded back to the travel rack where her baggage waited. Desiree contemplated the packed cases, then looked at the lush softness of the satin-sheeted bed. The bed won. She didn't have the energy to look for a nightgown tonight. She released the towel from around her shower-warmed body and slid gingerly under the covers. After turning off the bed light, she sighed with relief for having remembered to hang the "Do Not Disturb" sign on her door and telling the switchboard to hold any calls. She drifted slowly toward sleep as the pills she had taken began to do their work. With any luck she would be back to normal for her early meeting with Z.T. Maxwell, she mused hopefully just before surrendering to the sweet cloud of slumber surrounding her relaxed body.

Morning brought the blinding bright sun and a remarkably clear head. Stretching her slender arms lazily, she gazed about her bedroom, savoring the smooth feel of the sheets against her skin and the richness of her suite. If this were a sample of the life she would have during her stay, she was glad Laura had pushed her into selling her new line. Taylor/Maxwell just might not be so bad after all, she decided with a smile as she tossed back the covers. It only took a few minutes for her to find her aqua lace robe in the largest of her four cases. Drawing the deeply ruffled negligee about her nakedness, she reached for the phone to order breakfast. Having missed dinner the night before, she was more than prepared to do justice to a Texas-style meal.

She ate on the terrace, lingering over a cup of coffee

and gazing out over the Galleria area of Houston. Six miles from downtown, according to Z.T.'s very efficient secretary, it was Houston's second-largest concentration of office space, employing some 50,000 workers. It was here that Taylor/Maxwell had its headquarters. It was also where Desiree was to meet the head man himself.

Realizing her appointment time was drawing near, Desiree placed her empty cup on the table and rose. Taking a breath of the warmly scented air, she inhaled the rich essence of the city. There was success here, a pioneer spirit and friendliness that was evident even to her. A tingle of excitement feathered along Desiree's golden skin.

With springy, catlike grace, Desiree glided toward the closet where she had hung her clothes while waiting for her breakfast to arrive. The bright splash of emerald silk beside her favorite white Irish linen suit drew her eyes. The vivid color was an example of her new street wardrobe and was just what she needed to begin the first day of her temporary lifestyle. It was as totally unlike her normal public image as it was possible to be. For as long as she could remember she had suppressed her emotions, feeling somehow threatened by their very existence in her carefully controlled upbringing. She usually chose elegant cool colors, using them to perpetuate the image she had been taught from childhood. She had cultivated her slow, lazy ways to hide the incisive intelligence that was hers from birth. But for her time here, she intended to change all that. An imp of mischief stirred to life, recalling the fun of long-ago school days when she and Laura had shaken up the system too many times to count. That same hint of danger bubbled in her veins now, lending a golden gleam to her usually serene eyes.

Recalling her appointment, Desiree cast a quick look at her travel clock, frowning at the advancing hour. If she were to make that all-important good first impression, she had better get in gear, she scolded herself.

Rushing through her morning ritual, Desiree managed to dress in the time remaining before the limousine was due to pick her up. She paused before the full-length mirror to study the finished image of the last hectic hour. A doubtful furrow marred the dew-soft perfection of her face as she surveyed her unconfined hair. Silver brown waves rippled in a tousled shower to her shoulders, accenting the clean sweep of her cheekbones and emphasizing the heavily lashed shape of her incandescent green-shadowed eyes. She fingered an errant curl lying softly against the open emerald collar of her blouse, startled by the sleepy-eyed sexuality reflected in the mirror. Did she really look like this? she wondered, her gaze tracing the unbuttoned V at her neckline and the golden fullness outlined beneath the vivid silk. The conservative linen suit with its matching white heels and handbag was anything but businesslike without the sleek sophistication of her usual chignon.

She shook her head, tossing her curls into further disarray. No, she couldn't go to a business meeting like this. What was wrong with her intelligence? Z.T. Maxwell would take one look at her in this get-up and promptly decide her fantasies weren't dreams at all, but an extension of her own experience. She grinned wickedly, suddenly enjoying the deliciously uninhibited freedom of that thought. So what? Wasn't this just what she wanted? You bet, honeychild, she assured her image with a devilish wink of mischief.

The elevator ride to the elegantly appointed lobby was a smooth glide to the ground. As Desiree strolled toward the wide front entrance of the hotel, she was conscious of the admiring glances following her progress. This was fun. Her lips curved into a tiny smile of delight. Houston was definitely good for her. She hadn't felt this much excitement since she and Laura had replaced the paprika with chili powder in cooking class at the ripe age of ten.

Desiree stepped out of the cool air conditioning onto the carpeted walkway that led to the street. Instantly she was enveloped by the humid warmth of the morning. Being accustomed to Atlanta's unbelievably hot summers, she barely noticed the change as she glanced curiously about her. Sunlight bounced off tall, glassed office buildings, intensifying the heat and the extraordinary color of the city.

"Madam."

Startled by the low-toned prompting of the doorman, Desiree saw the silver limo that had brought her from the airport glide to a stop at the curb. The man at her elbow escorted her like royalty the few steps required to reach the car, opened the door for her and placed a light, impersonal hand under her arm to help her enter.

With the muted click of the lock, Desiree found herself enclosed in a plush cream leather cocoon. Protected by tinted glass windows and the opaque partition between her and the driver, Desiree had nothing to do but view the scenery and think about the upcoming meeting with her new boss.

Zackery Taylor Maxwell, Z.T. to his employees according to Laura. Age forty-one. Started just out of college with the family's widely known national firm. Got a reputation for shrewd business dealings and futuristic thinking. By the time his father retired Z.T. was a force to reckon with. His takeover had heralded the beginning of Taylor/Maxwell's assault on the international market. Now his network of stores numbered sixteen, most in the major capitals of the world, places like London, Paris, Rome, Venice, Rio de Janeiro, New York, Montreal and, of course, Houston, the corporation's home office.

Laura had been a fount of information on Z.T. although little of what she said had anything to do with the man's personal life. Other than that he was not married and never had been, she either knew nothing or she wasn't telling. Until this moment, Desiree hadn't realized the strangely blank area. Probably, Zackery Taylor Maxwell was one of those ambitious, hard-driving executives like her father who believed all work and no play makes Jack a very rich, successful man. Jarred by the thought, some of Desiree's excitement ebbed. While she was pleased to let go some of her inhibitions, she was not and never intended to be ready for the high-powered business world. She knew first-hand what a life like that did to people.

"Ma'am?"

The slow, drawling voice at her side jolted Desiree out of her rebellious thoughts. Glancing up at the patiently waiting chauffeur who held the door open for her, she smiled apologetically. Giving him her hand, she allowed him to help her from the car. Mentally chastising herself for having been caught unaware twice, she pulled herself together. She may not want to emulate her parents' lifestyle, but she had absorbed enough about business from her father and corporate law from her mother to know she'd better be on her toes for this meeting. Once signed, this contract was binding both to her and Taylor/Maxwell, and after having spent the better part of a week scrutinizing every word of the copy she had received in the mail, Desiree knew just how true Z.T. Maxwell's business reputation was.

Mentally gearing herself for the upcoming conference, Desiree entered the small, tastefully furnished reception area of Taylor/Maxwell. A well-groomed middle-aged woman smiled pleasantly when she stopped before the information desk and gave her name.

"He's waiting for you, Ms. Beaumont. If you'll just take the smaller elevator to your left. It's the top-level administration's private lift."

After thanking her informant, Desiree headed for the elevator. It was only a moment before the doors slid open to reveal a slender, dark-haired woman. "I'm Marsha James, Z.T.'s private secretary," she said pleasantly.

Desiree was startled at the identity of her escort. This woman, the owner of the brisk telephone voice that had snapped out orders like a battlefield commander, seemed too young for a position of such importance. She couldn't be more than twenty-eight, if that.

Hiding her thoughts behind a polite smile, Desiree followed her guide down a rust-colored carpeted hallway to a wide oak door standing slightly ajar. Moving quickly through the cream, gold and rust-colored outer office, the secretary stopped at a set of double doors to knock briefly before pushing the panels open.

Hesitating in the doorway, Desiree's eyes flickered

over the spacious room and its unusual transparent outer wall which framed the bright Texas summer day in vivid detail in spite of the protection of sun-tempered glass. Her gaze halted for a split second on the dynamic Houston skyline before settling on the two men facing her. With the light behind them, most of their features were lost to her eyes, yet she found her gaze riveted on the taller of the silhouettes.

Gliding languidly across the seemingly endless expanse of carpet, she assessed his tall frame through the thick screen of her half-closed lashes. He had to be an inch or two over six feet, she decided with a strange sense of *déjà vu*. Her gaze traveled appreciatively over the gray custom-tailored suit, coming to rest on his superbly tanned face. Halting next to the off-white visitor's chair, she suppressed a gasp as a shock of recognition shot through her. It was the man she had visualized in her dream. She stared silently into his deep brown eyes to find him staring at her intently.

Standing her ground before the assessing sweep of Z.T. Maxwell's gaze, she felt a warning flash in her mind at the power emanating from him. Here was a man who looked back at the world and defied it to beat him. Zackery Taylor Maxwell saw what he wanted, assessed what he had to do to get it, then reached out to collect his prize. Unconsciously, Desiree drew her cloak of cool nonchalance tightly about her in defense. Keeping her tawny green eyes fixed on his face, she saw the surprise in his expression give way to a brief flare of admiration before the businessman in him took over. A polite impersonal mask wiped the betraying reaction from his features.

There was danger here. Desiree felt it in her every nerve. Her wary senses were attuned to the aura of success surrounding him. He was everything she disliked in a man. He was another highly successful executive like her father and Jeremy. She should have been repelled . . . should have been, but wasn't. For beneath the polished exterior lurked a physical attraction in the most basic primitive level. Desiree felt it and was astounded at its force. There had been men after her divorce but never one to arouse this depth of response in her so rapidly. It was the dream . . . it had to be, she assured herself.

With a barely perceptible hesitation, she extended her hand. "Mr. Maxwell," she greeted, making full use of her slow husky drawl. She needed time to evaluate this new threat and she would use any tactic to get it.

Zackery nodded, a brief dip of his dark head. Sunlight danced across the gleaming sable-silver sideburns that framed his face as he enfolded her slender fingers in his large grasp for a moment, then released them.

"Ms. Beaumont, welcome to Taylor/Maxwell." He gestured to the man at his side. "This is my lawyer, Harold Sims."

Desiree acknowledged the introduction with a brief smile before settling slowly into the plush contours of her chair. Shifting ever so slightly, she searched for and found the most comfortable position, then raised her gaze to find both men seated and observing her every move. The undisguised male interest of Sims was in direct contrast to the watchful look in Z.T.'s eyes.

Crossing her legs with a whisper of nylon, Desiree relaxed with apparent indifference.

Zackery, too, lounged back in his seat, seemingly at ease in the midst of the tension between them. His gaze stayed locked on hers for a long moment, probing, searching for a crack in the barrier Desiree had erected.

From the safety of her indolent shield, Desiree followed his thoughts more easily than he could have guessed. She had a quick brain and an uncanny ability to read people—which she had honed to a rapier-sharp skill—hereditary gifts from each of her parents that she used too infrequently to suit that ambitious duo. She was well aware that her appearance and lazy manner were deceptive. Today she was grateful for the paradox she presented.

There was irritation in the tiny flare of Z.T.'s nostrils and the almost imperceptible tightening of his lips as his lingering scrutiny failed to produce any effect. Desiree saw the minute betrayals with relief. So far, so good, she congratulated herself silently. Her protective camouflage was still intact.

"Have you had a chance to go over our contracts?" he questioned, moving straight to the issue at hand.

"A little," Desiree replied, feeling a tiny surge of excitement at the duel she knew was to come. Although the contract selling her line to Taylor/Maxwell had been generous, there were two conditions attached which she had no intention of accepting.

Zackery nodded, a quirk of his lips indicating her answer was what he'd expected. "In that case, I think it would be good to have Harold go over the terms with you, so you'll have a full understanding of what's involved."

Desiree controlled a desire to smile at the carefully worded suggestion. She'd caught the faint emphasis on full understanding. So he thought he was dealing with a typical dreamer artist—and a woman at that. This was getting better all the time.

"I would appreciate it," she murmured with an

apologetic smile. She glanced at the lawyer, raising her lashes to give him the full benefit of her helpless appeal.

The poor man cleared his throat twice while giving his employer a harassed look which was ignored. "Yes . . . um . . . let me see." He paused, took a deep breath and fastened his eyes on the lengthy document he held. "Why don't I just read this and explain as I go along," he offered, keeping his head bent.

Coward! "That would be perfect," Desiree purred, almost laughing aloud. Her amusement died when she caught Zackery's sharp-eyed look. Oh no, girl, she chided herself, don't give the game away yet. It's too much fun. Dropping her lashes, she hid the challenging sparkle in her eyes as Sims's dry voice intoned legal phrases in the quiet room.

While giving the appearance of listening to the party of the first part, exclusivity and terms of agreement, Desiree analyzed her behavior. The imp of mischief driving her she recognized easily enough. It had been a long time since she had given in to it. Yet she had succumbed without a qualm to the allure of creating havoc regardless of the risk of exposing herself to the shrewd eyes of Z.T.

She paused in her mental examination, suddenly seeing that she'd been purposely flirting with danger, seeing how far she could go and still escape detection. She studied the figure behind the desk, wondering why she felt a need to provoke this male. Logic would say she should be in retreat . . . yet she wasn't. If anything, her actions bespoke a strange form of advance. In a way, she was demanding he catch her if he could. Was that the answer? Did she want Z.T. Maxwell?

Her eyes traced the sharp planes of his experience-lined features. Her gaze snagged the coffee-rich speculative stare. She sucked in her breath on a soft gasp. Yes, she did want him. The sight of him stirred a deep part of her she knew existed but had only touched in her dreams. There was an aching need uncurling in the pit of her stomach for the stroke of those long fingers. Giving in to the demand of Zackery's compelling eyes, Desiree lifted her protective screen for one tiny heartbeat of time. The most elemental communication between man and woman sizzled across space, blotting out the trappings of civilization. A dark flame flared to life in a shared meeting of the desire reflected in her honey green eyes.

He wanted her!

She touched the tip of her tongue to her lips.

His gaze caressed the moistened curve before returning to speak to her again. Not now.

The flame died as the executive mask settled in place.

Desiree dropped her lashes, retreating once more.

". . . escalating percentage based on overseas market reception. In conclusion, the name of Dream Magic and all designs created by its designer during the time limit set forth by this agreement shall be the exclusive property of Taylor/Maxwell Corporation without reservation." Harold Sims laid down the sheaf he held and looked up hopefully. "Have you any questions?"

"I do," Desiree answered crisply, her lazy manner disappearing as the analytical side of her nature took over. Speaking directly to the lawyer, she enumerated her objections in clear, precise tones. "One, I do not wish to be personally involved in any promotional campaigns, regardless of the media used. Two, I've never designed sleep linens in my life and there's a big difference between creating nightgowns and dreaming up a pattern for sheets, bedspreads, comforters and so forth. Not only is this line of products well out of my range, but I simply don't see the need in this case. Finally, the terms of this contract, if I sign, leave me with no alternative but to make my home here in Houston for quite some time, if not permanently. I'm not sure I want to do that."

Faced with this unexpectedly brisk summation, Harold Sims hesitated, glancing to his employer for guidance.

Desiree followed his gesture, locking Z.T.'s expression with an alert, unblinking stare.

A twist of Zackery's firm lips was the only sign he gave of the snow job Desiree had pulled, although there was a disturbing gleam flickering in the fathomless depths of his eyes.

"Let's take your reservations one at a time, shall we?" He held up a well-shaped hand, indicating the first of Desiree's list. "There was never any definite mention of your being used in our advertising, only a possibility."

"A possibility I would prefer didn't become a fact," Desiree interrupted determinedly.

"Why?"

"I prefer my private life to remain as it is. Any publicity of me as a person is bound to affect that. I agreed to sell my designs, not myself," she explained firmly, more than prepared to give up his lucrative offer if he wouldn't delete this clause.

The room was silent as Zackery studied her carefully. "Either I back down or you back out, right?" One dark brow lifted, punctuating his perceptive reading of the issue.

"Yes," Desiree agreed, a nod of her tousled head emphasizing her decision.

Zackery flicked his lawyer a glance. "Strike it," he ordered, ignoring the shock on the other man's face.

He turned, impaling Desiree with narrowed eyes. "About two," he began in a voice several degrees softer than it had been.

The change was a clear indication of his mood, and infinitely more effective than a shout. Desiree felt his iron will trained on her. Her senses surged to attention at the challenge. She disliked losing every bit as much as she suspected Z.T. did.

"I see no reason to believe you won't be successful at creating the linens to complement your gowns and negligees. While I know we have more experienced personnel to do what I'm asking of you, there's no one here who has your touch." It was Zackery's turn to stand firm. His flat statement as well as the poised strength of his seated figure said as much.

Putting up a token struggle flashed through Desiree's mind, only to be banished the instant it was born. It really mattered very little in the scheme of things. If she couldn't produce what Z.T. wanted, she knew he would get someone else to do it for her.

"Your point," she murmured, using the game term to give him his victory. "Now for number three."

"The tiebreaker," he challenged with a grin.

"Let's hope so," Desiree retaliated, not to be outdone. Out of the corner of her eye, she caught the swivel of the attorney's head as he tried to keep pace with their negotiations. A smile tugged at her lips at his befuddled expression.

Zackery glanced at his companion, then back to Desiree. His dark eyes gleamed with amusement. "In the interest of future relations, how about a draw?

We'll amend the clause to read that if the designer can't settle in the home office area, then by mutual agreement of the other two parties, another city shall be chosen." He sat back, blatantly pleased with his masterly handling.

Desiree suppressed the laughter bubbling within her at his tactic. Businesswise, he had been fairer than she had expected. She felt no hesitation in agreeing to the new terms.

"It's a deal," she pronounced in a soft drawl which signaled the end of her exertions in the commercial world—for the time being, at least. She had a feeling her days of doing what she wanted, when she wished, had ended. Zackery Taylor Maxwell had just purchased a sizable chunk of her life.

"Good." Zackery flipped back an immaculate cuff to check the time on his expensively thin gold watch. "I think lunch to celebrate is in order."

3

~~~~~~~~~~~~

Lunch?" Desiree questioned in surprise, one delicate brow arching.

Instead of answering immediately, Zackery turned to his lawyer. "You will join us, won't you, Harold?" It was a flat statement, not an invitation.

The attorney smiled apologetically as he rose, placing the amended contracts in his briefcase. "Only for a drink, I'm afraid, Z.T. I've got another appointment at one o'clock, so I won't be able to stay for long."

Zackery glanced back across his desk, a smile creasing his sharply defined features. "I guess it'll be just the two of us. I took the liberty of reserving a table at Tony's." A faintly teasing light entered his deep brown eyes. "If anything can convince you to make your home with us, it'll be Tony's food."

Alerted by the underlying personal message she sensed in Zackery's innocent-sounding words, Desiree searched her mind for a graceful excuse. Given her initial physical response, she wanted time to adjust to this new element in her life before finding herself confronted with Z.T. on a social level. "I hadn't planned—"

"—on being invited out?" Zackery interrupted smoothly, deliberately misunderstanding her quiet refusal. "All new partnerships deserve a toast, don't they, Harold?"

Harold cleared his throat and shrugged. "Of course, Z.T." He stared at her earnestly. "Tony's is one of Houston's finest establishments, more like a private club, Ms. Beaumont. You'll enjoy it."

"I'm sure I will," Desiree observed at her most languid, while giving her new boss the full benefit of her unusual eyes. Feeling outmaneuvered without being sure why, she made no effort to hide her thoughts from the man watching her so intently.

For a moment their gazes fused, hers questioning his motivations, his offering the reassurance she needed. It really was a celebration lunch. The physical attraction between them? That too, but only if she wanted it. No pressure.

A smile widened the generous curve of Desiree's lips and she flowed effortlessly to her feet.

Zackery followed suit, moving around his desk to her side. "Ready?" he asked, his head inclined toward her in a gesture that conveyed a certain degree of intimacy.

Desiree nodded, allowing him to cup her elbow and guide her toward the door. The warmth of his hand penetrated the linen of her jacket, suffusing her skin with miniature explosions of sensations. The feel of him walking beside her somehow pierced the natural space barrier she always maintained around herself. Her entire body was touched by him. His scent teased her senses, his faintly musky maleness calling to the woman buried deep within her. She should have felt threatened by the intensity of her body's instant knowing of this man. Instead she was challenged, stimulated by him and the danger he represented—awareness mixed with excitement. On the one hand there was an urge to lean into the tall frame which had invaded her personal isolation. Yet the sane, cautious side of her nature demanded she subdue her spiraling emotions. Dream or no dream, she hardly knew the man, and he was technically her boss. In fact, she had yet to address him by his first name or even Z.T., which most of his employees appeared to use.

By the time Sims finished the drink toasting their new venture, that last condition no longer existed. Zackery's deep-toned invitation to call him Z.T. had rumbled across Desiree's ears almost as soon as they had taken their seats inside Tony's. Limited by the attorney's quiet presence, Desiree had bitten back her personal aversion to initialed nicknames and agreed. Unfortunately, some of her reluctance must have shown through, she realized on seeing the brief frown that had marred Zackery's face for a moment.

"You seem to have something against my first name," Zackery observed accurately the second they were alone. He lifted his sharp-eyed gaze from the glass of Scotch and water he held to probe Desiree's expression. "I don't suppose you'd like to tell me why?"

Desiree's brow arched satirically at the seemingly innocent question cloaking a very clear demand for her reasons. She shrugged lightly, her tawny green glance holding his with deceptive ease. "It's not your name I object to, it's those initials. You sound like a movie mogul," she explained honestly.

Surprise flitted across his face. "Well, we're not going to spend the next few years being Ms. Beaumont and Mr. Maxwell," he growled in soft warning.

Desiree smiled slightly, veiling her lashes to conceal the amusement his obvious irritation stirred. "Where I come from, you would go by Zackery Taylor or Zackery T.," she offered, deviltry coloring the liquid tones of her slow drawl.

"No way," he shot back immediately, planting his glass on the table with a restrained thud. "Sounding like an American president or an old southern colonel doesn't appeal to me a bit more than Z.T. does to you."

Desiree's lips trembled as she tried to control the laughter bubbling within her.

"I suppose Zackery T. is all right. It matches Dee Dee a whole lot better than Z.T. does." The authentic rich western accent dripped with meaning.

Dark lashes flew open, revealing Desiree's startled reaction. "Dee Dee," she echoed in disbelief. "Dee Dee!" She drew herself up, all her languid poise shattered at the atrocity being committed on her name. "I have never been called Dee Dee in my life." The measured emphasis of her every word reflected golden sparks of gathering annoyance in her unusual eyes.

Deep brown pools of innocence flowed over the smoldering embers of her normally well-controlled temper. "Never?" He sighed dramatically. "Such a pity, ma'am. Where I come from we always shorten our womenfolks' names." He gazed at her solemnly. "Whatever are we gonna do?"

Indignation at herself for allowing Zackery to bait her into losing her composure and sheer amusement at the way he had accomplished his revenge for her comments about his name warred within her. Blast him for being so adept at penetrating her barriers, she thought with an inward groan of frustration. Her smile dissolved into a grin. But, oh what a man, her fanciful self purred in retaliation.

"I think we'd better compromise," she suggested. "I refuse to go through this contract stuck with the appellation of Dee Dee." She shuddered artistically. "Even if I could stand it, my French grandmother would turn over in her very proper grave." Her face assumed a mask of contrived horror. *"Sacré Bleu!"*

Zackery's eyebrows climbed at her murmured curse in theatrical French. He raised one hand in the age-old gesture of surrender, his eyes alight with masculine amusement as well as a gleam of something Desiree couldn't quite put a name to. "I give up. I'll offer my lady a deal. You may call me Zackery and I shall let your esteemed relative rest undisturbed. I'll abandon the offensive Dee Dee in favor of the deliciously unique Desiree."

Not sure whether it was wise to comment on the provocation of Delicious Desiree, she contented herself with a regal inclination of her head.

The frivolous beginning of their lunch together was her undoing, Desiree realized later that afternoon. Aided by the private intimacy of Tony's atmosphere, Zackery had had no trouble in breaching her usual defenses with his appreciation of the absurd. An hour meal had stretched to two. By the time he had handed her into the company limo for an initial foray into apartment hunting, Desiree was ready to admit her original concept of Zackery's cold, businesslike image needed some rethinking. However, the full extent of his expertise didn't dawn on her until she stood wrapped in a damp towel in front of her hotel closet, searching for something to wear when Zackery picked her up for their dinner date.

"Damn," she swore with soft vehemence, her hand hovering between a classically simple champagne silk wrap dress and one of Manuelo's newest brainstorms, a delicate blush pink number in wispy chiffon. She eyed the frothy creation skeptically. It had been a farewell gift from her old boss who had assured her it would do wonderful things for her. She hesitated a moment, undecided about the image she wished to project. She should choose the more conservative dress—it was safer—but the filmy teardrop halter gown would be so much more fun. And definitely more eye riveting, her dreamer self whispered. With a reckless smile, Desiree selected Manuelo's present. What's a little harmless flirtation? she assured herself.

Sighing in pleasure at the sensuous touch of the light drifts of fabric against her freshly bathed and scented skin, Desiree slipped into the form-clinging chiffon. While she made up her face, she considered her approach to the hours ahead.

Honest by nature, she had no hesitation in admitting her attraction to Zackery. All things being equal, she would have been delighted to pursue the chemistry existing between them. However, things were definitely not equal. That was the rub. Not only was Zackery her boss—although, to be precise, that was a minor irritant easily handled with the use of proper discretion—but he, in spite of his very real charisma and pure masculine charm, was one of the breed of men devoted to business and its pursuits. He was just like every other man in her life to date—successful, and going places with a shrewd eye for making a deal and reaching the top.

No, intelligence and logic demanded she guard against this new invasion in her life. Past experience and knowledge gained through painful encounters with top-echelon executives had alerted her to the signs. She was eager to indulge herself, but not to the foolish—not to mention self-destructive—extent of getting personally involved with one Zackery Maxwell.

She rose, casting a final glance over her finished image. The richly feminine allure of her reflection in the mirror startled her slightly as she studied the vision of Manuelo's genius. The featherlight ripples of chiffon floating about her slender body created an illusion of beauty for her fine-boned features. The soft tint of pink was a perfect foil for the unusual shading of her eyes and hair. Tonight she had decided to subdue her tousled first impression by sleeking her curls back from her face to a point just behind her ears. Secured by a delicately fastened silver band, the remaining ash brown waves framed the back of her head in a shining halo of silken curls. Tiny diamond earrings shimmered against the honey tone of her skin. The flawless jewels echoed the deep teardrop plunge of her neckline, exposing the smooth satiny curve of her breasts. Strappy silver sandals complemented the long slender legs below the frothy foam of the gown's ruched hemline. Satisfied with her image, Desiree reached for the matching, ruffled tricornered scarf as Zackery's knock announced his arrival.

When she opened the door a smile curved her lips at his punctuality. "I was half expecting cowboy boots," she drawled, employing the teasing banter they had established at lunch to set the evening's mood. Her eyes slipped appreciatively over Zackery's silver gray European-cut suit before settling on his dark face.

A smile crinkled the corner of his mouth and let the velvet-eyed stare make a similar survey of her own elegantly gowned form. "I'd thought about it, considering where we're having dinner," he commented, glancing down at the polished Italian leather shoes he was wearing.

"Oh?" Desiree stepped back, gesturing for him to come in. "Are we going country?"

He shook his head, his grin widening. "Are you ready?" he questioned, making no move to enter her suite.

Intrigued by the hint of mystery she sensed in his refusal to answer directly, Desiree nodded. "Do I get a clue?"

"No." He chuckled, taking her arm. "However, I do promise to tell you something about the city that's going to become your home for a while, at least. Provided, of course, you found an apartment." He shot her a curious look as they waited for the elevator.

Desiree grimaced disgustedly. "Not yet. Have a heart for this poor Atlanta girl. In spite of my very helpful driver," she paused to add in an altered tone. "By the way, thanks for the use of your car."

He shrugged dismissively before ushering her into the elevator. "It's yours until you get settled," he explained matter-of-factly. He ignored her surprise. "Houston's a big place. It'll be easier for you until you get your bearings."

"Are you always so generous with your new employees?" Desiree asked, her voice clearly skeptical.

"Nope," he drawled laconically. "Only with very special people." His glance flowed over her composed features, warmly intimate in the close confines of the empty compartment.

For a split second, caught unawares by the mercurial change in Zackery's mood, Desiree's poise deserted her. Her gaze locked on his face, her breath whispering through slightly parted lips. Desire—alive, vibrant and demanding swirled about them, the pulsating throb growing stronger with each heartbeat. Zackery lifted his hand to touch her cheek. The tender gesture was reminiscent of her dream. Entrapped by the masculine spell and the fantasy of her own mind, Desiree swayed toward the beguiling warmth of his body.

"Desiree." Her name on his lips was the call of a sorcerer. His dark eyes held her mesmerized. The real world dissolved into vague shadows without substance.

"Who are you?" Desiree whispered, her gaze chained to his expression. So many emotions were locked up inside her, begging for freedom. So many barriers lay unbreached. Yet in this magical moment, Zackery touched the very essence of her being. She knew it, she felt it . . . she wanted it.

"Only a man," he breathed in a husky murmur.

She sighed deeply as he drew her against him, spreading his legs to support her weight. Her hips pressed into his and she could feel the pulsing maleness of him stirring to life.

A moan of excitement and longing escaped her throat as Zackery lowered his mouth, his warm, firm lips brushing hers gently at first. One hand slipped under her hair to the nape of her neck while the other pulled her inexorably closer.

Desiree's lips parted eagerly beneath his confident

and complete possession. His tongue flowed in her mouth like molten honey, filling every secret place and wrapping around hers in a silken bond of ownership.

Desiree felt the tremors shaking her body from the raging blast of desire Zackery had ignited. She heard her own soft purrs of delight with a sense of unreality. Nothing mattered. Only the sensation of Zackery's warmth fused with her own, and the aching needs of her yearning.

"Come home with me, little one," Zackery rumbled near her ear while nibbling at the sensitive area behind it. "Come, let me show you how good it can be for us."

The total assurance in his offer reached Desiree through the mist of fantasy and physical pleasure enveloping her. The blaze of passion froze and she went still as reality shattered the glorious illusion.

"No," she denied him through suddenly dry lips. She wedged her hands between their molded bodies. "No."

Zackery was breathing unevenly as he looked down at her. "No?" he echoed in disbelief. "Why?"

Desiree pushed against him until he released her. "Because I don't want to," she stated flatly, forcing her voice to utter the lie.

At her uncompromising words, his hands fell to his sides, his stare probing her features, seeking an answer to the barrier she had erected between them. He opened his lips to speak but was thwarted by the elevator easing to a halt at the lobby.

Desiree sighed in relief at the respite the next few moments offered. She had almost succumbed to Zackery's masculine allure once again, she acknowledged, annoyed at her inability to resist him. Hadn't she learned anything in the past few years? Here she was going all weak-kneed like an impressionable teenager or a love-starved divorcee. What a laugh. She was neither.

There had been a few relationships since her marriage, but conducted only on her terms. While Jeremy had awakened her to the passionate side of her nature, he had also shown her just how vulnerable it made her—and she had wanted no part of that kind of defenselessness again. So she chose her companions with care, opting for a safe, restrained pairing that offered no threat to either her or her lifestyle. Until now. Her feelings toward Zackery were anything but restrained.

"Why?" Zackery's quiet demand cut through the silence stretching between them.

Desiree turned her head from the study of the passing night-shrouded streets to trace Zackery's set profile. She'd been so lost in thought, she'd hardly been aware of being escorted to his unusual Talbot sports car waiting at the curb. The expensive fragrance of genuine leather filled her senses as she took a slow calming breath. The muted glow of the flickering streetlights produced a strobe effect in the close confines of the car.

He cast her a quick glance when she failed to answer. "Well, I'm waiting," he prompted, his tone showing no traces of his recent arousal. "Why did you draw back?"

"It was too soon," Desiree hedged, debating whether to be as blunt as he apparently was determined to be. After all, they'd be working in the same building, if not in the same office. Maybe it would be better to get things out in the open now.

Zackery frowned thoughtfully, obviously turning her short answer over in his mind. He shook his head, frustration replacing his expression of concentration. "No, it's more than that. You weren't saying not now." He paused to study her perceptively before returning his attention to the traffic. "I think you meant not ever."

Stung by the certainty in his voice, Desiree's decision was made for her. He was right, so why not give him the reasons he sought? "You're very sharp," she affirmed with deceptive calm. "I don't want to get involved with you."

"Why? Because you're working for me?" he asked mildly, his voice conveying little more than polite curiosity.

"No, at least not directly." Desiree spread her hands in a purely Gallic gesture used to express the unexplainable. "It's your way of seeing things, reacting to them. Your type puts everything on a debit and profit sheet. I don't want to be a statistic."

Zackery's hands tightened on the steering wheel, a visible sign of his rising temper at her blanket condemnation. He guided the sleek, cream-colored Talbot into the parking area of their destination and switched off the engine. Turning to her in the softly lit glow of the restaurant's outside lights, he raked her with an irritated glare.

"So I'm sentenced without even the courtesy of a defense?" The last came out on a muted roar of an annoyed male.

Desiree stood her ground, not in the least intimidated by his temper. "I can recognize a man like you a mile away. That aura of power around you betrays you every time and I sure don't need long to recognize the chemistry between us," she shot back indignantly.

"If there had been any dry timber around, we could have started a forest fire."

The astounded silence that followed her rebuttal lasted all of three seconds before Zackery's deep-throated laughter filled the car. Desiree stared at him in bewilderment.

"What's so funny?" she demanded crossly, not finding anything remotely amusing about her comment.

"You are." Zackery chuckled, leaning forward to drop a light, almost brotherly kiss on the tip of her nose.

Desiree drew back, eyeing him balefully through gleaming slits of annoyance. "Explain, please," she questioned with all the finesse of a sharp claw ripping through delicate silk.

Zackery's laughter faded, although his dark eyes still reflected his appreciation of the situation as well as a distinct touch of admiration. "You've been a surprise from the moment you walked into my office. After seeing those drawings of yours, I'd expected a very sexy lady." He paused, his gaze traveling slowly over her slender body braced against the passenger door. "What I hadn't anticipated was the sharp brain to go with the package. And I sure didn't expect our chemistry"—a choked-back chuckle punctuated his use of Desiree's word—"any more than you did." He frowned faintly, his mood altering suddenly. "As for tarring me with the same brush as every other man you've known, I object."

"Well, I didn't think you'd be pleased," Desiree retorted, relaxing her rigid posture somewhat.

He nodded. "No man would be," he agreed dryly. "However, I will admit I haven't handled this situation with much polish." He lifted his hands in a small gesture of apology. "I assure you I'm not usually so clumsy. I'll do better in the future."

"Clumsy? Future?" Desiree exclaimed, appalled at the blatant assurance in his pronouncement. "There is no future—haven't you listened to a word I've said?"

"Sure I have, Dee Dee." He mimicked her slow drawl to perfection. "But if I may point out, no one in his right mind would leave a possible fire hazard untended." He opened his door to get out. "I was a Boy Scout, you know."

"The only scout you were was for Sitting Bull at the Little Big Horn," she muttered irritably as she slid out of the car.

Zackery grinned, taking her arm in a light grip. "Feeling surrounded, are you?"

"Only mildly," she purred sweetly. "After all, being from Atlanta has its advantages, honey. We know all about sieges and fires. We survived them both."

Zackery's fingers tightened possessively for a moment. "We'll see."

He drew her down the walkway leading to a rustic log cabin. A lantern light cast a warm glow over the rough-hewn entrance and softened the raw-timbered walls.

"Where are we?" Desiree murmured. The unexpectedness of their destination provided a badly needed subject change. Zackery's blatant refusal to acknowledge her withdrawal left her with very few options.

"We, my dear visitor, are about to enter La Tour d'Argent. The perfect setting for us both."

Desiree's brow lifted in mute inquiry as he pushed open the door.

"Where else could you find such a blending of two nations, the classic French cuisine and service of your heritage combined with the traditional American setting of Houston's oldest log cabin?"

Desiree glanced appreciatively around the room, expecting an incongruous mixture of cultures, only to find a warm, gracious atmosphere reminiscent of a European hunting lodge. Animal trophies, antlers, old oil paintings and pictorial china, along with antique copper kettles and an early twentieth century upright piano added to the cozy atmosphere. Leaded, stained glass windows, displaying the restaurant's tower logo and the *fleur-de-lis*, decorated the first floor. Following their hostess upstairs, Desiree found the cabin's former bedrooms had been converted into intimate lounge areas. French music played softly in the background, lending a continental note without interrupting the conversation of the guests.

"What do you think?" Zackery asked after the waiter had brought their wine and departed.

Desiree smiled teasingly. "I guarantee you we don't have anything like this back home. If I weren't sitting here, I wouldn't have believed a place like this were possible."

"I've lived long enough to know anything's possible," he murmured. Zackery lifted his glass, his gaze tracing the pure, clean outline of Desiree's features. From the wide, oddly shaded eyes more often than not hidden by her absurdly long lashes, down the slender, aristocratic nose to the fullness of her generous mouth.

"Stop it, Zackery. I'm not a candidate for what you have in mind, remember?" Desiree chided, raising her wine to her lips and allowing a tiny sip to ease down her throat. Zackery's visual seduction was a potent force dragging her ever closer to the moment of truth.

One masculine brow rose in pretended hurt. "I

can't look?'' The sensual tenor of his deep voice completely destroyed whatever innocence lay in his intentions.

Desiree's eyes flared to life, flashing their golden emerald challenge across the small, intimately lit table. "No." Flat, uncompromising—yet she knew her words were wasted. Zackery needed more than that, just as she did herself. What lay between would not be resolved on a verbal level. Their answer lay beyond that. Desiree sensed it and she knew Zackery did as well.

He touched his glass gently to hers, the restaurant crystal ringing with the deep tone of a brass bell. "To dreams, fantasies and realities."

4

No you won't, Zackery Taylor Maxwell." The sleepy mumble emerged from beneath a snowy pillow. Desiree groped her way out of her tangled position to glare at the buzzing alarm clock. The only good thing about being awake was that she could leave Zackery's plaguing image behind. One slap of her hand brought silence, but not the calm serenity she craved. That had been ruined last night and the night before by her now-you-see-him-and-wish-you-didn't boss.

Desiree slipped from her rumpled bed, vividly recalling her current predicament. "Arrogant . . ."—she padded across to her bath to begin her morning ritual—" . . . demanding . . ."—she started to brush her teeth, glaring at her reflection in the mirror. "Oh, he makes me so angry," she muttered through a froth of minty foam. She rinsed her mouth, almost slinging her toothbrush into its holder with temper. "The whole staff is bound to think something is going on between us. Blast his interfering! Why couldn't I just have a regular office like every other designer? Why did he give me that damn fancy setup across the hall from him?"

Receiving no answer to her irate questions either from her sphinxlike employer or from the silent bathroom, Desiree stepped into the shower, still seething with her sense of ill-usage. It was bad enough being stuck way up in the rarified air of top-level management without the added burden of gossip that Z.T.'s latest move was bound to generate.

In the two short days she had been exposed to Zackery, her life had been altered almost out of all recognition. Even her lovely, leisurely baths and her sunrise sketch sessions were victims of Zackery's dynamic energy. She didn't have time for any of it; Z.T. Maxwell had seen to that! Now it was a rush just to get to work on time.

Slipping quickly into white brushed denim slacks, Desiree reviewed her schedule for the day. After her eight o'clock breakfast, the limo would arrive to take her to work by nine, then there was lunch with the head of fabric design at noon, a meeting with the pattern department at two and finally the limo would return to pick her up at four for apartment hunting.

"Damn!" Desiree's oath coincided with room service's knock. Casting an irritated glance at the rapidly moving minute hand on her clock, Desiree hurried through the sitting room, fastening the remaining three buttons on her primrose cotton shirt.

Breakfast was a quick affair while she finished dressing. She arrived downstairs in the lobby at the appointed 8:45 pickup time looking much more cool and relaxed than she felt. Her driver's friendly smile showed a distinct gleam of masculine admiration which soothed away some of her ruffled temper.

"Good morning, Ms. Beaumont," he greeted her before glancing at the brilliant sky overhead. "It's gonna be another scorcher."

"Probably," Desiree agreed absently, more interested in arriving at the office on the dot than in the weather. The car door clicked shut, closing her in a quiet shelter where she could take a much-needed breather before she reached her destination.

After the bombshell in the form of a private office suite complete with secretary that Zackery had waiting for her on that first day, she wanted to be prepared for anything. The unbelievably personal and possessive attitude he had taken still astounded her. Given his no-nonsense public image, she'd been unprepared for such blatant tactics during business hours. She had neither anticipated having her design area on his floor nor having almost unlimited authority in the creation of her Dream Magic line. It was this combination of circumstances that had ruined her sleep and left her with an empty sketch pad this morning. Having Zackery make his attraction to her clear over dinner was bad enough, but having Z.T. Maxwell show his interest to the world was close to being paralyzing. That would never do.

Private offices indeed! Idiot. He might as well have taken out an ad in the company newsletter stating his intentions. Desiree frowned, thinking of the gossip she knew was bound to follow his uncharacteristic behavior.

The limousine slid to a smooth halt beside the porticoed employees' entrance, ending her musings before she had developed any real plan of action. Summoning a smile in gratitude for the chauffeur when he came around to help her out, Desiree stepped onto the sidewalk. Her expression froze in place on seeing a trio of women eyeing her arrival curiously and whispering among themselves. One she recognized as a senior secretary on the top floor.

So it had begun. Giving no hint of the anger building within her, Desiree strolled nonchalantly toward the glass doors, nodding politely as she passed her huddled coworkers. With every step she took to the elevator, then down the hall to her office, she railed at Zackery's clearly possessive attitude and her own loss of composure. Nothing about this job was going as planned. Desiree had the sensation of being on a collision course with Z.T. Maxwell—with no possible escape. Only the long years of hiding her true feelings kept her face serenely undisturbed. Her habitual indifferent mask was never so impenetrable. Inwardly she might rage against the man who seemed bent on adding her to an undoubted line of willing females, but she had no intention of betraying that fact to anyone, least of all him.

"Good morning, Mary Beth." Desiree entered her suite, pausing at the sleek, modernistic desk to greet her secretary.

"Ms. Beaumont," the younger girl returned shyly, a tentative smile adding a touch of life to her ordinary features. She pushed her wide-rimmed glasses more securely on her short nose with a nervous gesture. "Z.T. wants to talk to you as soon as you get in."

He does, does he! "Let me put my handbag away," Desiree remarked blandly, sauntering across the rich thickness of dove gray carpet to her own office.

Yesterday the cool perfection of pearlized colors

accented with touches of creamy yellow had delighted her senses in spite of their proximity to Zackery, while the functional simplicity of the clean lines of the furniture had created an illusion of unlimited space. Today the pleasure she had taken in her surroundings was dimmed by the scene downstairs and her own inner turmoil. How safe and calm Atlanta was in comparison to Houston. No Z.T. to keep her balanced on the knife-edge of attraction. No office tattle-mongers whispering about the new hotshot designing sexy lingerie and her special place on the executive floor with the boss instead of being in the design department with the rest of her kind.

After dropping her purse in the large bottom drawer of her desk, Desiree relaxed in her chair for a moment, gathering herself together before going to Z.T.'s office. She stared thoughtfully at the phone. For two cents she'd walk over to her drawing board and forget all about Z.T.'s message. She glanced sideways from beneath her lashes, eyeing the innocent tilted table and its high stool perch. No, that was the coward's way. Besides, she had a sudden urge to lock horns with her aggravating employer, she decided with a brisk nod of her carefully groomed head. The memory of those women downstairs still rankled and it was his fault she was in this situation.

Punching the appropriate buttons, Desiree quickly reached Zackery's extension. The calm voice of his secretary was only a shade warmer than Desiree's own as she stated her reason for calling.

"Desiree."

Zackery's dark velvet tone in her ear brought back images Desiree wanted to forget. Scenes of the dinner they had shared flashed in her mind, the burning tracings of his gaze, the lingering whisper of his words.

Firmly subduing her unlooked-for responses, Desiree leaned back in her chair.

"You left a message for me to call you," she reminded him expressionlessly.

A faint sigh echoed across the wire. "So you've heard," he stated, a hint of impatience edging his comment. "I think you'd better come over here. We need to talk and I want to see your face while we do."

Desiree grimaced at the unwelcome order. "Now?"

"Yes." The terse affirmative was followed by an abrupt click as the line went dead.

She stared at the silent phone in her hand, wondering at the temper she sensed in Zackery's manner. She replaced the receiver on its hook with a resigned shrug, stood up and gave one final glance at the partially finished design, Golden Temptress, clipped to her sketchboard. It didn't appear she would complete her newest fantasy this morning as planned.

"I'll be in Z.T.'s office," Desiree explained, stopping at Mary Beth's desk on her way out. The formalities taken care of, Desiree took the short walk necessary to bring her to Z.T.'s inner sanctum. Marsha James gave her a faint smile as she motioned Desiree to go on in.

"Here I am," Desiree announced, gliding across the space to the visitor's chair she had occupied for the first time only three days before.

Zackery rose, his dark eyes following her unhurried movements. "That was quick," he observed, resuming his seat after she'd taken hers. "I half expected you to keep me dangling for half an hour."

Crossing her legs in a relaxed movement, Desiree cocked an eyebrow, acknowledging his thrust. "I thought about it, but I wanted to get back to Temptress so I decided to come now," she elaborated, self-mockery evident in her answer. "I have a meeting at twelve. . . ." The pointed reminder drew a frown of irritation.

"I know. I set it up, remember?" Zackery's clipped reply left Desiree in no doubt of the success of her baiting. He leaned forward in his chair, resting his elbows on his desk. His eyes probed hers, the dark depths carrying a warning gleam too pronounced to be ignored.

"I think it's time you and I came to an agreement."

"So?" Desiree prompted warily, wondering which one of several tactics he'd use to try to gain whatever it was he wanted now.

"I realize I've been rushing you and your work. I realize, too, you're a lady who likes everything slow and easy and I've ruffled your fur the past couple of days with my requests."

Requests, ha! Desiree thought, remembering the decisive tone with which each of his orders had been given.

"You know as well as I do the importance of speed in the production of a unique line. The longer we're hung up in the initial phases, the greater the chances are that someone will slip up on security." He paused to give Desiree a chance to comment. When she didn't, he continued. "However, it appears my efforts to protect your work have caused some problems and I want to set the record straight so we can work together as a team. I hired you to design for Taylor/Maxwell. I did not hire you for your feminine appeal. Nor did I locate you on this floor to have you under my thumb, in my bed or over some of my more senior employees. You are where you are only because the security on this level is tighter than anywhere else in the building. Everyone who works here is carefully screened and, in most cases, has been with us for years."

Knowing Zackery was right should have soothed Desiree's irritation, and it did slightly. But the position she was in still remained and she saw no way of solving that. "Surely you didn't expect your arrangements to go unnoticed," she responded dryly.

"I knew it would be commented on, yes," he admitted with a brisk inclination of his dark head. "What I hadn't banked on was our mutual interest to complicate the situation nor—"

"Mutual what?" Desiree retorted, the sheer masculine certainty in his statement raising her temper several notches. "I never said I was—"

Zackery quelled the rest of her protest with a commanding gesture. "I didn't anticipate the spread of talk through the staff," he concluded as though she hadn't spoken. "Pure and simply, your line of lingerie intrigued me as well as most of my department heads. From a business point of view your talent could make us all a lot of money. That is why you are placed as you are. The *only* reason," he emphasized firmly. He sat back, obviously ready now to listen to her comments.

Desiree studied him thoughtfully, weighing his words against her own perceptions of the man. One slender foot enclosed in an oyster gray slingback sandal swung in a gentle arc as she considered the situation. There was no doubting the sincerity of Zackery's explanation. Yet . . . ?

"Why couldn't I have had an office in design? Surely you could have worked around the security problem more easily than furnishing a place for me up here?" she asked, coming straight to the point. "I would have thought an arrangement like that would have been more acceptable to everyone."

Zackery's expression remained an unreadable mask as he fielded her blunt question. "I want this line to be the best thing Taylor/Maxwell has ever done. The potential here is tremendous and I want every phase of its evolution to be scrutinized and honed to the absolute. Ever since I saw the first set of drawings, we've had buyers out scrounging this country, Europe and the Orient for fabrics; we have cutters and seamsters standing by; our talent people are searching for just the right girl to represent the concept." Dark fires of determination smoldered in the gaze locked on her. "And you, Desiree Beaumont, have got to be where the action is. It's your fantasies we're bringing to life. They exist nowhere else but in your mind. I want them—every last one of your visions. For the duration of our contract, you are mine."

Desiree felt the full force of Zackery's dynamic personality in his final claim of ownership, an ownership which seemed to mean more than just the business aspect they were discussing.

All of her independent spirit rose in rebellion over the totality of his possession. She was no man's property. She never had been, she never would be. Yes, she had sold her ideas for lingerie to Taylor/Maxwell; yes, she intended to give the best that was in her to create her illusionary sleepwear—she wanted to see the real-life gowns every bit as much as he did. But not at the expense of her freedom. She would not be shackled by anyone, least of all this man.

Molten sparks of fire showered the jade in her mutinous eyes. Yet her voice carried no hint of the swirls of rebellion growing within her. Instead it was a whisper-soft statement of a woman sure of her own power and confident of her defenses.

"I belong to myself, Zackery. My personal allegiance begins and ends with me. You own Dream Magic only. What I do, the sketches I complete, the gowns that finally result—all of those are yours." Unafraid, Desiree raised her lashes to their fullest, daring to defy him. She would not back down. "The mind that envisions them is mine." Correctly interpreting the territorial gleam in Zachery's eyes, she added a final decree. "I am my own person, now and in the future. Regardless of my association with you."

Desiree knew Zackery understood her reference by the tightening of his features. Suddenly their business discussion had changed. The attraction each felt sizzled in the silent room. By her own words, Desiree had purposefully given it life and breath. Zackery had laid his cards on the table; now it was her turn. She would be neither pushed nor led into a relationship until she was ready. If she ever was.

Stare for stare, Desiree matched him, the glitter of her eyes against the strength of his appraisal as it battered, probed and tested, searching for her slightest weakness. Desiree watched him, unmoved by the relentless assault. Her barriers were impregnable and she knew it. Her father, her mother and even Jeremy had taught her well. She understood big-business dynamics through her sire, she knew the force of a woman's ability to blank out her emotions from her coldly logical mother and she knew the devastating consequences if she failed from her time with Jeremy. Yes, here in this office, on this ground, she was secure.

Abruptly Zackery abandoned the visual duel for

another tactic. "Will you have dinner with me to-night?"

"No." Desiree's reaction was cool, even mildly amused. "I thought we had sorted all that out the other night," she added, deliberately ignoring the way he had overridden her then.

A twisted grin marked her blatant omission. "I think not," he pointed out in a suspiciously conversational tone.

Desiree shrugged delicately. "I'm a harried working girl who still hasn't found an apartment." She glanced at her watch. "I've less than five hours to do two days' work, then I must jump in a car and hunt for a place to lay my poor head." Never had her accent been so affected.

"Touché." Zackery chuckled, acknowledging the hit. "What if I offered to help you in your search?"

Catching the subtle inflection in Zackery's teasing suggestion, Desiree eyed him narrowly. Surely he had more finesse than this.

He laughed outright at her unconcealed suspicion. "You don't trust me an inch, do you?"

Desiree shook her head, subduing an urge to join in his amusement. The beguiling sound of his deep masculine humor teased the corners of her lips until they quivered. The dancing gleam sparkling in the dark depths of his eyes invited a response. Suddenly she could control herself no longer. Silver ripples of laughter harmonized perfectly with his own rich notes.

With this sharing, some undefinable emotion wafted across the space between them. Touching, retreating, tantalizingly just out of reach of Desiree's sensory hold. Her gaze caught and held Zackery's. The echoes of mirth faded into the nothingness of unneeded sounds. For a timeless space, Desiree willingly opened her defenses, drawn by the alluring call of this man. A second sooner or a moment later, there was danger. Yet here, now, it was right.

"Have dinner with me . . . please." Zackery's command was a velvet plea, catching her at her most vulnerable. Memories of her dream, their kiss, the dinner they shared called to her. Demanding, yearning, they would not allow her to refuse him his request. Had he commanded, she would have been able to.

"Friday." She surrendered on a sigh. "I really am too rushed today."

He inclined his head gravely, breaking but not shattering the fragile spell. "Friday at seven," he agreed. He rose and came around the desk. He studied her face intently. "How much longer are you going to keep me dangling?"

Desiree gasped softly at the audacity of his demand. Leave it to him to cut straight to the heart of the matter. Yet his bold honesty appealed to her. With him, there was no need to guess at his intentions. "Days, weeks . . . forever, maybe," she retaliated daringly.

Zackery extended his hand. She took it, allowing him to draw her to her feet. They were inches apart physically, fused by their thoughts and separated by their emotions.

"I'll give you time . . . for now." He lifted his free hand to curve around her throat while he searched her expression. "I've never waited for a woman in my life."

Desiree's lashes fanned languidly shut for an instant. Instead of being put off by Zackery's stark statement, Desiree found it triggered an equal honesty in her. She felt no need to hide behind the age-old games women play against men. She opened her eyes, letting Zackery see the indecision in her mind. "I don't sleep around. I never have and I never will. I also don't make commitments. I walk alone, I live alone and every once in a while I take someone into my life." She paused, knowing she had to make her position clear. "But only on my terms. You're different. You have been from the first and I'm out of my element. . . ." Her voice drifted into silence, leaving him to draw his own conclusions.

For a long moment, he studied her without speaking. Then Zackery raised his hands to frame her face, gently, possessively. "I'm going to kiss you, Desiree. You know I want much more than that, but I'll wait for the rest."

Zackery lowered his head slowly, allowing Desiree ample time to protest or resist if she chose. She did neither. She wanted his touch, she ached to experience the magic that was his alone. She slid her arms up his back as he leaned closer, his mouth only a breath away. She felt the whisper of it against her lips, tantalizing, teasingly just out of reach. Staring deep into his eyes, she read the desire, the urgency to know and to explore. Caught in the challenge of his male mystery, Desiree's lips shaped, parted to receive him, while her eyelids slowly lowered to seal her in a fantasy of sensory pleasure. She inhaled his rich male fragrance, savoring each subtlety, the expensive cologne, the faint trace of fine materials, but most of all him. Without maidenly coyness, Desiree revealed herself in the full spectrum of a woman's generosity. Sharing an intimacy with Zackery, giving . . . taking. Equal partners, skilled in the tactile sensations so special to the art of lovemaking.

For a brief moment, Desiree lost all sense of her

place in the universe. She simply felt. The taste of Zackery lingered in her mouth, vibrantly alive, as he slowly withdrew his lips from hers while still cupping her face in his hands.

"I think that was *not* a very good idea," he murmured huskily, the velvet throb in his voice evidence of his heightened awareness.

Desiree fought to control her breathing, a little shocked to find herself panting as though she had run a mile. "I don't suppose you'd let me back out of dinner tomorrow night?" she questioned half seriously when she was sure she could speak clearly.

Zackery's fingers tightened in gentle warning. "No way. We've exchanged promises. A gentlemen's agreement, if you like."

Desiree lifted her hands to his, releasing his hold with careful insistence. "We have?"

He nodded, allowing her to break the contact between them. "Contract: I will not push you into my bed. Proviso: You will go out with me." He leaned back against his desk, a complacent grin tugging at his lips. He crossed his legs, obviously awaiting her reaction. He didn't have long to wait.

"I never agreed to any such thing," Desiree denied immediately. "I accepted one date . . . that's all. If you think that kiss entitles you to . . ."

Zackery glanced pointedly at his watch. "I thought you said you had a busy morning," he interrupted in a suspiciously neutral tone.

"Oh, I do." Desiree smiled sweetly, stifling her temper. If she had a rolling pin handy she'd cheerfully clunk him over the head with it. Her eyes gleamed with deviltry at the sudden image of him fleeing before her as she brandished her weapon.

"Hey, come back from wherever you are."

Zackery's command drew Desiree's startled glance. "I didn't think a kiss could send you off in a daydream. Unless, maybe, it has inspired you," he challenged.

"It's done that, all right, but not the way you mean," Desiree drawled mysteriously, moving to leave.

"I don't think I like the sound of that. I don't suppose you'd like to elaborate," he hinted, remaining where he was.

At the door she turned, striking a calculatedly seductive pose. "Not now, Zackery. I'm a working lady under contract. My boss doesn't like time wastin'."

Zackery pushed himself away from the desk, showing every indication of taking up her dare. "I could give you the day off."

Desiree shook her head in mock regret, knowing he wouldn't mix business with whatever might be between them. "I'll tell you on Friday," she teased in a breathy purr, before opening the door and strolling unconcernedly out. The smile on her lips widened at the barely audible oath which was silenced by the closing of the heavy panel behind her.

The round-eyed surprise on the oh-so-correct Ms. James's face only added to Desiree's enjoyment as she headed back to her office. The euphoria her skirmish with Zackery had produced lasted her through her very hectic day. It even survived three uninspiring but perfectly adequate apartments that afternoon.

Arriving back at her suite much later than she had expected, Desiree made do with a sketchy meal ordered from room service and a quick shower before tumbling exhaustedly into bed. She was asleep from the moment her head touched the pillow. Mentally and physically tired, she slumbered dreamlessly, undisturbed by Zackery's vivid image or her own creative fantasies.

Friday morning was a rushed repeat of the day before, with one notable exception. She managed to finish her sketch of the Golden Temptress. The intercom buzzed just as she put down her pencil to study the completed drawing. Frowning at the interruption, Desiree slid off her high stool and went to the desk to answer Mary Beth's summons.

"You asked me to remind you the car would be here an hour earlier for that sublet appointment," her secretary explained.

The furrows on Desiree's brow deepened as she glanced at her watch, realizing she had been working nonstop since lunch.

"Okay, Mary Beth. I just have to put my things away, then I'll leave. Would you call downstairs to the receptionist and see if he's arrived. If he has, ask her to let him know I'm on my way."

Minutes later she scanned her office, checking to be sure that she had left nothing of importance unsecured. Her completed sketch had been rolled up and placed in the special locked compartment Z.T. had had installed, while her discarded ideas were tiny shreds of paper in the waste can. She glanced down at her slightly wrinkled self with a faint sigh. She wished she had time to go back to the hotel and change. The soft cream lutesong tunic she had chosen this morning to team with the cocoa velveteen jeans would just have to do. Running a hand over her hair in its elegantly restrained chignon, she was reassured to find that the silver brown mane was still impeccably groomed. After collecting her suede handbag, she left her office, locking the door behind her.

The precautions Z.T. had drummed into her head

yesterday were too strong to be ignored. Business espionage was an accepted fact of life in her field as in many others.

Desiree stopped at her secretary's desk. "Is he downstairs yet?" She didn't relish waiting around in the lobby until the limo arrived. Not only would she be forced to endure the speculative glances of the receptionist as well as anyone who passed by, but she would be advertising her use of Z.T.'s car.

Mary Beth nodded quickly, a hesitant smile curving her lips. The admiration and awe she felt for her boss showed clearly in her bright blue eyes. "Yes, Ms. Beaumont. He'd just driven up when I called back."

Desiree studied the girl Z.T. had forced on her, really seeing her for the first time. She was struck by the eager, puppylike devotion in her expression. "Are you new here?" she asked curiously, ignoring for the moment the need to keep to her schedule.

Some of the animation died in the younger girl's face. "I was one of the junior secretaries for Mr. Hunt in personnel. This is my third week," she admitted quietly.

No wonder she looked ready to leap for the door every time anyone walked in, Desiree concluded in grim humor. "How old are you, Mary Beth?"

Dark lashes flickered nervously. "Twenty, just. My father is the security chief for Taylor/Maxwell." Pride filled her tacked-on offering.

Desiree smiled gently. "No wonder you were chosen to be my watchdog. You probably know more about screening my visitors than I ever will."

At Desiree's compliment, Mary Beth's ordinary features lit with a broad grin, the first completely natural reaction Desiree had seen. "If I don't, my dad'll have my hide," she confided. "This is Mr.

Maxwell's very special project." She nodded her mousy head, emphasizing that statement.

The mention of Z.T. reminded Desiree of the limo waiting for her and her date with the man himself. She was already late for one and if she didn't hurry she was going to be even later for the other. That would never do! After a quick word of gratitude for her young assistant's help during the last few days, Desiree hurried for the elevator.

5

Blast!" Desiree swore as she squirmed to get a better grip on the recalcitrant zipper jammed midway up her spine. Unruly curls tumbled about her face and across her forehead to brush annoyingly against her eyes. Irritated, she exhaled a couple of fierce breaths, momentarily clearing her sight. Although the good it did was debatable as she wriggled more desperately to extricate herself from her champagne silk trap.

A brisk knock at the door was the last straw. That could only be the ever-punctual Zackery.

"Damn," she exploded, giving up. She stalked through the sitting room, clutching the slipping edges of the skimpy, strappy bodice with one hand behind her back. It was his fault she only had forty-five minutes to dress, so he could just make himself useful by getting her unstuck.

Throwing open the door, she glared belligerently at the dark silhouette of her escort. In the split second before she spoke, she catalogued the chocolate brown suit, the lighter shade of the matching silk shirt. Understated, undoubtedly expensive as well as elegant, it was a perfect foil for her own outfit. That is, if she ever got the damn thing on.

"Don't just stand there grinning," she commanded irately. "Get me out of this . . ." She waved a hand graphically at her half-on, half-off gown.

Zackery grinned wickedly. "Honey, when you decide to capitulate, you don't mess around, do you?" he drawled seductively, stepping inside the door and shutting it noiselessly behind him. "I do think we'd be a little more comfortable in your bedroom, however." He tipped his head to one side, awaiting her explosion.

Desiree's eyes narrowed, a sure sign of her rapidly escalating temper. "If you had any concern for that hide of yours, you'd refrain from ruining what's left of this evening," she informed him with feeling. "You know very well what I meant, so don't try anything."

"A challenge, Desiree. I would have thought a woman of your years would know better than to go around daring a man."

"A promise, Zackery Taylor." She flowed around in a smooth pirouette, presenting him with her back. "Now will you please undo this zipper?" She glanced over her shoulder, wondering at his hesitation. The warmth of his inky gaze as he visually caressed the bared expanse of her back made her catch her breath. Her annoyance melted away as though it had never existed.

His hands curved around her shoulders, turning her toward him. "You're a glorious creature, Desiree Beaumont," he rasped, drawing her against his chest.

Desiree tipped her head back, studying the clean line of his features. "We'll be late," she offered in a husky protest, the jade in her eyes swirling over him with unconscious invitation, the gold offering a promise of untold delight. This is what she wanted, what she had waited for, she realized suddenly—the feel of his body against hers.

"Do you care?" The deep words carried a more serious underlying demand.

Desiree considered that, aware of the significance of his question. Nothing had really changed between them. Her senses were more alive, more demanding than they'd ever been in her life. The metamorphosis was shocking and she hadn't had time to adjust and, until she knew what she wanted, she would not, could not afford to give herself to Zackery.

"My senses say no I don't," she replied finally, honestly. "My mind still isn't sure." She waited, knowing as he did that he could command her body. She felt the tension in the long muscled length of him. Knew he wanted to make her respond to him. Yet she knew he would not. He was not a man to take what was not freely given.

"You are an able opponent." He sighed, relaxing slightly. He stared into her eyes, his fingers tracing the delicate bones of her shoulders. "You fascinate me, do you know that?" The rich tones of his deep voice curled about Desiree's body, stroking her skin with unseen caresses. His hands dipped lower, smoothly pushing aside the tangles of shoestring straps.

Caught in the mesmerizing quality of his slumbering gaze, Desiree made no protest. She felt the restraint in him which had been absent before. Feeling safe, she gave herself up to the delight of his touch.

His mouth lowered to hers, warm, moist, exquisitely gentle. The undemanding pressure teased at her parted lips, making no effort to enter. The heat of Zackery's hand as it closed about her breast drew a moan of pleasure from her throat, which he caught in his own mouth. The intimacy of his gesture kindled a flame deep within Desiree's being. Pressing her body against his, she slipped her arms up his back, forgetting her clutching hold on her dress.

Released from her tight grip, the fragile silk slithered to a delicate drape at her hips, leaving her upper body bared to his eyes.

"You're playing with fire," Desiree warned, arching her neck to allow Zackery full access to the honeyed skin of her throat.

"I don't mind getting burned," he breathed against her flesh as he trailed a sensuous path down to one rosy-peaked breast, swelling in anticipation. "I promise not to let the fire go wild." His tongue curled possessively around the button-hard nipple as his mouth drew with gentle urgency on the velvet mound cupped in his hand.

Desiree's lashes fluttered shut as the delicious temptation he offered washed over her. To play with a flame, to court a passionate danger without fear of the consequences was a challenge the woman in her was unable to resist.

"That's it, my sensuous cat . . . purr . . . scratch. You're as safe as you want to be," he encouraged.

The husky demand unfurled the hidden desire in her. Desiree dug her nails into Zackery's shoulders, clinging, catching at the expensive rough silk of his suit. Suddenly she hated the fabric barrier separating them.

"You're not playing fair," she whispered, sliding her hands beneath the collar of his jacket and pushing it down his arms. Sometime during their embrace, the fastenings had been released. She neither knew nor cared which one of them had done it.

Zackery moved back slightly to shrug out of his coat. Desiree's fingers slipped dexterously along the line of tawny pearl buttons starting at his waist, and she finished with a deft tug at his tie, releasing the perfect knot at his throat.

A twisted smile softened the sharp cast of his features, his eyes crinkled with masculine amusement. "You do that very well," he murmured as he drew her bare breasts against his sable-furred chest.

Desiree rubbed her body deep into the thick pelt, delighting in the deliciously rough rasp of the heavy curls against her swollen mounds. "You don't like it," she teased, using her lips to brand him with her own form of possession.

His low groan of appreciation marked his arousal. "Give me back my promise, witch, and I'll show you just how much," he demanded, his fingers weaving a tantalizing pattern over her stomach.

Desiree inhaled a soft gasp of awakening need. "An agreement is an agreement," she reminded him in a throbbing moan of escalating desire. "Besides, what about dinner?"

"To hell with contracts and food," he growled, rearing his head back to stare at her. "I want you now and I know I'm not alone in what's happening."

Desiree heard the urgent desire and sensed the hair-trigger masculine instinct behind it. Forcing her emotions to obey her, she sought to stem her own body's demands. This wasn't part of the bargain. She wouldn't give herself to Zackery yet, not until she was certain in her mind exactly what he wanted from her. With him, she sensed that a bed, a passionate flame would not be enough. Her intuition told her this man could mean more to her than any person had ever meant. But did she want more? Did he?

"No, Zackery," she answered in a voice still husky with her own needs, "I hold you to the letter of our agreement."

For a critical moment, she thought he was going to ignore her. His hands tightened obstinately.

"You expect us to sit down to a candlelight dinner for two—*now?*" Hot molten brown eyes poured out a passionate denial as Zackery stared at her in stunned amazement.

Knowing what she was asking of them both, Desiree steeled herself against the alluring temptation of changing her mind. "Yes, I do." She met his eyes unflinchingly, knowing her own vulnerability.

"Why?" he demanded.

"You know why."

His fingers bit into her flesh at her continued refusal. "That idiocy about time?"

She nodded. "I won't be pushed, Z.T. Not by you, not by my own body," she countered. "Now do you want our date or not?"

One sable brow lifted at her clear ultimatum. "You really intend doing this to me." It was a flat statement of fact.

"And to myself, Zackery," Desiree reminded him softly, sensing the danger point was past. "You weren't the only one caught in the flames."

Zackery loosened his hold on her, sliding his hands to her hips where her dress rested. He eased away from her body, keeping his eyes on her face as he lifted the fragile silk to veil her glorious nudity. "I suppose I did ask for this," he admitted with a crooked grin of self-mockery. "I guess I'd better fix that zipper now."

Desiree smiled bewitchingly, catching the bodice of her gown in one hand when Zackery turned her around. "It would be nice to arrive at dinner in a better state than I am now," she agreed.

"I just wish my 'state' were as easily remedied," he grumbled as he slid the pull smoothly up her back. He reached across her shoulders to the bunched web of straps that held her dress in place. "Be still a minute and I'll tie you into this thing," he ordered, lifting the halter ends and fastening them behind her neck. "The sooner we're out of here the better I'll like it."

"Now Zackery Taylor," Desiree teased, moving away with a wicked sway to her hips.

He gave her a swift pat on her sensually undulating derriere. "Watch it, woman, or I won't behave myself," he growled half seriously.

Desiree slanted him a seductive glance over one bare shoulder. "Since your hair needs combing, I'll let you use the bathroom first." She laughed throatily at his disgusted expression as she sat down in front of the mirror to make up her face.

Picking up his jacket and tossing it on her bed as he went by, Zackery followed her suggestion. "You realize we're going to be late, don't you?" he retaliated, peering at his disheveled image. "How would you feel about dinner at my place?" He came to the door, buttoning his shirt.

Desiree caught his eyes in the mirror. "How should I feel? I assume you intend to remember our agreement?"

"Then you'll come?" He knotted his tie without removing his gaze from hers.

Desiree finished stroking on the bronze lipstick which complemented the shimmering gilded green eye shadow she had chosen. "Who's doing the cooking?"

He grinned slightly, his eyes flickering with amusement. "My houseman."

"I'll come," she agreed, rising to her feet. She glanced down at her nylon-clad toes. "All I need are my shoes."

She hunted in a closet while Zackery finished dressing, emerging with heels in hand just as he slipped into his jacket. He leaned against the door, watching her as she buckled the golden sandals.

"Ready," she announced.

A gleam of deviltry lit his eyes. He came across the room and took her arm. "I doubt it."

Exchanging a smile of perfect understanding, Desiree allowed him to escort her from the suite.

The drive to his apartment was much shorter than Desiree expected in spite of the busy streets. By mutual unspoken consent, their conversation centered on her newest sketches and their possibilities.

"You know, I think you should have called and warned your man," Desiree commented, strolling across the deeply carpeted hallway to Zackery's penthouse entrance.

Pushing open the sleek double doors, Zackery gestured her inside. "You don't know Vanderbilt. He prides himself on being on top of any situation. In fact, he would be highly insulted over a mere dinner for two."

"Good evening, sir . . . miss."

Startled at the intrusion of the halting voice, Desiree glanced across the black-and-white-tiled foyer to catch her first glimpse of the most unusual-looking man she had ever seen.

Easily as tall as Zackery, he had the face of a battered prizefighter, an image reinforced by heavily muscled arms and a stocky torso. Something about the stillness of the man at her side as well as the wary, defensive shadows in the pale blue eyes of the houseman warned Desiree to tread lightly.

A smile curved her lips as Zackery guided her toward the open doorway where Vanderbilt waited.

"This is Ms. Beaumont, Vanderbilt." Zackery's deep voice was expressionless as he made the introductions.

Desiree extended her hand, somehow liking the unusual individual before her. Expecting a heavy grasp, she found her fingers folded carefully into a gentle paw. "Zackery has just finished singing your praises and promising me you wouldn't be put out with us descending on you like this." She laughed teasingly. "I confess I'm starving to death. Will you truly take pity on us?"

Desiree's outrageous approach was rewarded with a weirdly twisted smile which further distorted Vanderbilt's odd composition of features. "I will bring the canapés in fifteen minutes, but dinner will take about an hour," he enunciated slowly, obviously conscious of his speech impediment.

She ignored the awkward sound, concentrating on the man. She was neither repelled nor offended by

Vanderbilt's physical appearance. Although a loner by nature, Desiree was surprisingly adept at seeing behind social masks. She recognized artifice as quickly as she appreciated humility and gentleness.

"Cheese puffs," Desiree suggested hopefully, naming her favorite predinner tidbit.

Vanderbilt inclined his head, some of the stiffness leaving his body. "I'll see if I can find a few lying around," he agreed before disappearing as silently as he had come.

"Thank you." Zackery curved an arm around Desiree's waist, turning her toward him. Dark eyes, fathoms deep, gazed down on her upturned face.

"For what?" Desiree questioned, one delicate brow arching in puzzlement.

"For not making Vanderbilt feel like a freak just because he was born the way he was." He dipped his head, brushing her lips with a kiss that held more gratitude than passion. "Even though he's been my houseman for years he's still very sensitive about meeting someone new."

Desiree curled her arms around his neck. "I don't usually judge people on the basis of appearance," she chided softly, enjoying the feel of Zackery's body pressed intimately against her. "I leave that kind of stupidity to others."

Zackery grinned at her tacked-on commentary. Slowly his amusement died, replaced by the searching probe Desiree was coming to recognize and accept. "Who are you, Desiree? Woman? Witch? Artist? Seductress? Or the solitary person I sense behind them all? Which is the reality and which is the fantasy?"

Startled by his perception, Desiree veiled her lashes. Suddenly she was weary of fighting him and her own body. Each time she had sought to cool the fire between them, Zackery had subtly switched tactics to find another vulnerable spot. In the short time she'd known him, he had learned more about her than anyone else she knew. In a strange way, she was glad. She wanted him to care enough to discover her secrets. But not too fast! She needed time to do her own searching.

"I'm only myself . . . Desiree," she evaded lightly, standing on tiptoes to give him a quick kiss designed to distract him from the subject before she moved out of his embrace. "How about a tour?" she suggested, hoping to further lighten the atmosphere. "I'm a fanatic about colors and textures, especially those not for public consumption. I think you can tell a lot about a person by the things they surround themselves with." She smiled at him expectantly.

"Tour?" Zackery echoed, momentarily confused by the abrupt change of subject. "You're not going to answer me, are you?"

She shook her head. "It's not in the agreement."

He sighed impatiently. "I'm beginning to hate that word." He glared at her quivering lips, easily reading the chuckle waiting for freedom. "I wouldn't advise it, woman. I'm not in the best of moods right now. You know why." He grabbed her hand and stalked into the wide, gracefully curved living room. A broad expanse of glass opened onto a wraparound terrace, giving a glorious view of the night-shrouded Houston skyline.

Desiree halted in the center of the uniquely modern lounge, her artistic eye drawn to the rich simplicity of the decor. Pearl gray walls curved around midnight blue suede couches and chairs. Touches of off-white provided the accent to complement several thick pelt rugs. The sensuous islands of fur partially covered an intricately inlaid wood floor. Potted greenery in the form of beautifully tended plants brought the outdoors in for the finishing touch.

"Through those doors to your left is the dining room and through here"—Zackery gestured to the hall on his right—"are the bedrooms. Would you care to see them?"

Desiree read the challenge in his words. Tipping her chin, she eyed him fearlessly. "With this as a sample, do you think I would refuse?" She lifted her hands in a fluid arc to encompass the appeal of her surroundings.

Zackery shook his head. "I just . . ."

"Besides, there isn't time before dinner anyway, so I know I'm safe," she interrupted complacently, casting him a deliberately provocative look through her half-closed eyes.

Zackery's hand tightened on her elbow. "Did anyone ever tell you you were a tease?" he demanded, slightly irritated. He reached past her to push open the door to the master suite.

Desiree turned to him, the tour forgotten for a moment. "Not yet," she admitted huskily. She ran the tip of her tongue over her bottom lip as she gazed deep into the smoldering embers of his eyes. "But I feel sure you're going to be able to if you keep on baiting me." She waited, lips parted for Zackery's retaliation. A flash fire of excitement heated her blood and singed every nerve with danger—a vital, daring, heart-racing duel of the sexes. His man to her woman. Suddenly Desiree knew what she wanted. She wanted Zackery—now for whatever time they had together.

Zackery slid his hands up to cup her shoulders. "A game, Desiree?"

"Not unless you make it one." She felt the web of

his will reach out to entangle her, hold her immobile. "I've been honest with you. It's my way, but that doesn't mean I know no other." Her warning was clear. He could now proceed at his own risk.

"And the stakes?" His whisper ghosted across the tiny breath of space separating them.

Desiree gave him a direct stare, matching her strength against his. "You surprise me," she commented, a tinge of sarcasm coloring her voice.

Zackery's gaze pinned her ruthlessly. "As you do me. A short time ago you stated you needed a breathing space. What changed your mind?"

"You did," she answered simply.

"How?" One dark brow lifted, emphasizing the demand in his question.

Desiree smiled secretly, ignoring his curiosity. She touched the tip of her forefinger to his lips. "I thought you were going to show me your bedroom." She stood easily in the tightening circle of Zackery's arms, feeling him resist to her prompting. He wanted to force her to answer. She sensed it with a surprising depth of certainty. Momentarily, she wondered at her own unusual behavior—her lack of inhibitions where Zackery was concerned, her sudden desire to plumb the depths of her own sexuality. It was as though by leaving Atlanta she had also left her aloof independent shell and had come into a world of thoughts and emotions she had only dreamed of.

"All right, you win this round," Zackery conceded with a wry twist of his lips. "But next time, it'll be my turn. I'm getting tired of having you retreat just when things get interesting." He released her slowly.

Undisturbed by the masculine threat, Desiree stepped back and turned to survey his bedroom. The first thing she noticed was the unusual deep dusty blue of two walls and the gleaming reflections of the windowed third in the mirrored fourth.

"Blue wouldn't be your favorite color, would it?" she teased, her eyes making a slow sweep of the rich cream rug, finally coming to rest on the focal point of the suite, the bed. On a raised dais, flanked by two steps, it dominated everything else. A sinfully luxurious fur spread seemed to stretch endlessly across the king-size mattress.

"I do like it," he admitted, watching her face closely.

Desiree barely heard his answer, her gaze held by the decadent pull of the gleaming animal skin. She glided toward it, her senses demanding she touch, stroke the seductive pelt. It was perfect and totally unexpected. In her mind's eye, she could visualize herself curled in the chocolate folds, her body wrapped in the gilded gold of her Temptress design.

"Is it real?" she whispered softly, almost reverently as she reached out to pet the velvet-smooth covering.

"Yes," he murmured, his voice deepening at her reaction.

Desiree lifted her eyes, the green in them never more vividly alive. "I think I'm not the only one with fantasies," she breathed.

Zackery nodded his dark head, obviously unsurprised by her odd choice of words. "I had a feeling that was where your ideas came from."

Desiree searched his face, trying without success to penetrate his mind. "How did you know about my dreams?" Shaken by his perception, she was powerless to summon the anger she would have felt at another's invasion of her innermost secrets. How easily he penetrated her defenses. Until now, only Laura had known where her ideas originated and that was because Desiree had told her.

"I don't know how I knew," he mused slowly, carefully considering his own feelings. He shrugged slightly, a hint of frustration in his expression. "I just did."

Desiree's lashes framed her unblinking emerald-and gold-flecked eyes as she stared at him. What was happening to her? she wondered warily. Why did she have the feeling her decision to enjoy all Houston had to offer was suddenly fraught with unforeseen hazards? The excitement, the danger, the challenge—they were still beckoning her onward, enticing her to risk, to gamble. But what was the wager? Was she overreacting by feeling that the game had suddenly developed a new, more intricate twist?

Zackery smiled gently. "No comeback, honey?" he drawled, lifting her hand from the fur on his bed and enfolding it in his warm grasp.

"I'm thinking." Desiree's comment was nothing more than the truth, although it served a much more useful purpose by making Zackery chuckle, thereby altering the strange aura surrounding them.

"Come on, designer mine, let's go see about feeding the inner woman," Zackery suggested, tucking her arm under his in a proprietary gesture. "You're going to need all your strength for this new life of yours."

"New life?" Desiree echoed, automatically following the pressure of his guiding hold. She eyed him askance, needing to know how he was able to crawl inside her head and unearth her dreams, intentions and expectations.

"Just how well do you know Laura?" she questioned, hitting on the only logical explanation she could think of for his mind reading.

He glanced down at her curiously. "I've met her a few times at parties, business dinners, that sort of thing. Why?" He released her arm as they stopped beside the suede sofa.

Desiree settled comfortably into the plush softness and crossed her legs before answering. She raised her eyes, intent on catching every touch of emotion on the sharp lines and planes of his face when she gave him her reply.

"Because I don't especially like the idea of you two discussing me," she stated flatly, her expression daring him to deny they had.

For a moment, Zackery's entire body froze, only the depths of his eyes conveying any hint of his thoughts. A brief gleam of anger? satisfaction? flared for an instant, then died.

"I've never discussed you personally with anyone. Least of all with your friend. My opinions are all my own, no one else's." He subjected her to an all-encompassing scrutiny. "I doubt that talking to Laura or anyone would have helped anyway. I think whatever path you choose is yours alone."

Off balance at his accurate summation of her personality, Desiree stared at him silently. And she had actually wanted Zackery to get to know her if he could. Ha!

She'd never felt more naked, vulnerable and defenseless in her life. Even Jeremy's impact on her had never produced the effect of Zackery's quiet analysis. She should hate him for his knowledge, for it gave him power over her that no one else had. Yet, strangely, no such emotion made itself felt. It was as though his words were all a part of their chemistry. Already written, they were as inevitable as the dawn following the black of night. He upset her, unnerved her, moved her to passion one minute and anger the next. Yet she was drawn to him by a force more powerful than her own will. She wanted him with a steadily increasing need. A desire which demanded appeasement . . . soon . . . now.

With his final reading of her, Zackery had unwittingly given her the freedom to accept him into her life. She could allow their relationship to burn itself out, knowing he would understand when she moved on—as she must, as she always had.

"You're not allowing me the breathing space you promised me earlier," she reminded him slowly.

He shrugged lightly before lifting a small silver tray covered with tiny golden balls. "I've changed my mind," he admitted as he offered her a choice.

Desiree bit into the warm tidbit. "Don't you think that's a little unethical?" she questioned casually as though they were discussing the weather.

Zackery placed the platter on the table at her elbow, then took a seat in the matching chair beside her. "Nope," he drawled slowly. "Just smart."

"We'll see," Desiree purred, curling more comfortably in her place. "We'll just see."

6

~~~~~~~~~~~~~~~~

That was delicious," Desiree commented. She leaned back in her chair with a faint sigh. She smiled at Vanderbilt when he glanced up from removing her plate, a grin quirking the edges of his mouth. "I especially enjoyed the Amaretto mousse—next to the cheese puffs," she amended hurriedly.

"We noticed," Zackery murmured wickedly.

Desiree veiled her eyes and turned to stare at him across the width of the steel gray slate table. "Now Zackery, you did promise to feed me." The honey sweetness of her voice matched the melting look she gave him. She heard Vanderbilt's smothered chuckle in the background.

Sharing a meal with Zackery in his home had made

her all the more aware of her own nature. He called to her body in a way that summoned forth her most vivid fantasies. The sheer magic of him and her own responses released her own sensuality. She flirted, she teased, she played, enjoying her new freedom. She was bold, wild and deliciously wicked. The tactily pleasing and visually stimulating decor of Zackery's apartment and their intimate dinner helped to create the dreamlike illusion.

Her about-face had succeeded far better than any plan or tactic she could have ever employed to disconcert Zackery. Had she been in the mood for revenge for the way he had turned her life inside out, she would have been amply rewarded. She had laughed inwardly as she had watched him struggle through the first two courses, trying to adjust to the new strategy. The sight of his uncharacteristic confusion had goaded her on to even more outrageous lengths. The result had been more bewilderment, shock, dawning comprehension, then outright retaliation with Zackery playing the impatient lover to her seductress.

"Would you like to take your brandy in the lounge?" Vanderbilt reappeared momentarily in the connecting door between the dining room and the kitchen.

Zackery nodded, rose and came around to Desiree's side. "I think he's trying to tell us something," he murmured, holding her chair.

Desiree flowed to her feet, subtly brushing her body against Zackery's. Her senses, heightened by the verbal foreplay over dinner, reacted immediately. She inhaled a soft gasp. "Don't you like his idea?" she asked boldly, her smile ancient in origin.

"Honey, believe me, I like it very much," he breathed against her ear. He placed a light, tingling kiss just below the tender lobe.

Desiree made no effort to control the delicious shiver that rippled across her skin. Instead she leaned closer to his warmth.

He curved his arm around her waist and guided her to the sofa where a tray bearing twin snifters of brandy awaited them.

"Why do I get the feeling you're seducing me?" Zackery murmured a few moments later when he took his place beside her, stretching his arm across the back of the couch. He ran his hand under Desiree's tousled curls to the vulnerable nape of her neck.

She swirled the amber liquid in her glass, a tiny smile teasing the corners of her mouth. She slanted him a glance loaded with reckless excitement and growing need. "Perhaps because it's true. Don't you approve?"

"I do, but I wonder what prompted your about-face," he replied whimsically.

"Let's just say I exercised my female prerogative." She leaned languidly forward to place her glass on the table in front of them. Talk about playing with fire, her coolly aloof self taunted in a brief, but unsuccessful, attempt to restore her sanity. She had a right to the physical excitement Zackery offered, didn't she? she argued in return. After all, they were both free, mature adults with no commitments elsewhere.

Settling her own small mental rebellion, Desiree relaxed against the cushions again, managing to slide nearer to Zackery in the process. The heat of his body enfolded her. The scent of his cologne mingled with the faint aroma of the brandy he finished in one final swallow, creating another strand drawing her ever closer.

"Desiree." The husky summons of Zackery's deep voice was his final binding tie.

Lifting her head, her lashes half closed against the sensations building within, Desiree gave in to the need to know the taste of him again. Slowly, savoring every bite, she traced the shape of his mouth with tiny, teasing kisses. Her fingertips slipped across the breadth of his shoulders, first with the faint pressure of unsheathed claws, then with soothing circles of gentle stroking. She felt him catch his breath at the dual feminine assault.

"I love the way you change your mind, woman," Zackery groaned as he curved her body tightly against his muscled frame.

Responding to the touch of his hands on her heated skin, she eagerly parted her lips, darting the tip of her tongue past his teeth to instigate the first duel of the mating game.

His mouth opened to receive her and she reveled in the passion awaiting her. His deepening desire incited her still more. Using her supple body instinctively, she twisted into his lap, pressing her breasts against his chest as she delved further into the male essence of him.

"My God, Desiree, you don't know what you're doing to me . . . to us," he rasped against her ear.

Zackery's hands on her back slid further down to the curve of her hips and beyond, his fingers clenching with escalating passion. Desiree shut her eyes against the need rising up to match her own. This was right, she acknowledged with sudden perception, in a way it had never been for her before. Whatever came after was unimportant in the face of that one blinding fact.

"We can't stay here," Zackery muttered thickly.

"What?" Desiree mumbled, startled out of her hazy golden world by a disoriented swirling movement.

Zackery lifted her high in his arms, bending his head briefly to seize her lips in a hard, demanding kiss. "You're beautiful." The throbbing compliment echoed the flaming admiration in his dark eyes.

A slow smile curved Desiree's swollen lips as she nestled against him, her arms curled about his shoulders, her cheek resting under his chin. She inhaled the musky scent of his arousal as he carried her into his dimly lit bedroom. He set her gently on her feet beside his bed.

He gazed deeply into her golden emerald eyes while his hands slipped to the halter fastening at the back of her neck and released it. Obeying the unspoken command in his visual communication, Desiree inserted her fingers under the collar of his coat and pushed it off his shoulders.

She felt the zipper at the back of her gown glide smoothly down when she untied his tie and pulled it free. Her dress floated to the floor followed by Zackery's shirt.

"I knew you'd be like this," Zackery groaned, drinking in the sight of her slender, near-naked form. His hands drifted lightly, caressingly across the honey-toned skin. "You feel like golden velvet slipping through my fingers."

Desiree swayed toward him, drawn by his touch and his words. Her breasts brushed against his richly furred chest as her hands made their own exploration of his taut male body. Firm muscles contracted in pleasure at the seductive stroke of her wandering fingers.

She reached for the buckle of his belt, needing fresh territory to investigate. The muted thud of his pants hitting the floor passed unnoticed as she absorbed the sheer power of his body.

Suddenly the roles shifted as Zackery swept her against him. His mouth closed over her aggressively, ravaging the soft inner moistness with awesome strength and a strange kind of tenderness. In moments their shoes and their two remaining scraps of clothing had joined the scattered pile on the carpet.

Without breaking the head-to-toe contact between them, Zackery drew Desiree down on the deep pile spread.

"Desiree, where did you come from?" Zackery grated, lowering his head to the valley between her breasts. "You're like no one I've ever known."

Desiree heard his whispered words, vaguely wondering at their meaning but too deeply submerged in the sensations he created to ponder them. Slipping deeper into the silky fur cradling her, she pressed closer to him. She moaned aloud as his teeth sank into a gentle suckling circle around one nipple.

"Zackery," she moaned, inflicting her own brand of punishment along the strong column of his neck.

At his name on her lips, Zackery lifted his head to stare into her heavy-lidded eyes.

"Has it ever been like this for you before?" he demanded arrogantly.

"No," she managed faintly, knowing they both deserved her honesty.

"I knew it," he breathed in satisfaction. "I knew it from that first day."

He dipped his head, beginning a trail of passionate biting kisses down the slope of her breast to the middle of her stomach.

Desiree's hands closed convulsively on his dark hair. "Oh!"

His fingers raked gently across her thighs, darting to the inside with short, arousing forays that brought her shivers of desire. Her legs shifted restlessly on the soft cover, setting off tiny explosions of feeling over her passion-sensitive skin. Her hands kneaded the muscles of his shoulders in an ancient mating rhythm.

His moist tongue circled her navel, sipping at the tiny well until she cried out in pleasure.

"You have the suppleness of a cat and I want to stroke every inch of your velvet hide," he growled against her abdomen. He rolled on his back, bringing her atop him in one smooth motion.

Desiree's lips sought the taut male nipples when she felt his hand slide down her spine, stroking the sensitive area at the base before prowling on to clench the curve of her hip.

She arched against him, her body seeking the aroused warmth of him, unconsciously fitting her smooth curves to his masculine shape. She felt the rigid tension of him as his maleness reacted to her provocation.

Then his mouth fastened on her breast, tugging, sucking, building a fire deep within her being.

Her neck arched as her head tipped back, the tumbled curls brushing her shoulders with teasing tendrils.

"Oh please, please Zackery," she moaned, responding to the demand of her whirling senses and his caressing hands.

"What is it you want, honey?" he demanded in a deep, throbbing whisper. His tongue soothed the nipple he held captive before repeating his assault on its twin.

"I want you," she pleaded as his mouth closed over her breast once more.

Driven wild by his loving punishment, Desiree dug her nails into his shoulders. "Zackery." It was a woman's command as old as mankind. It was time. The game was done.

"Desiree." His answering call came as he reversed their position, lifting his body high for their union. A touch of his knee made a space for him between her legs. Gathering her close, he claimed her with all the power of his body.

"Zackery!" she gasped, accepting him and enfolding her softness about him. Reveling in his embrace, her hands kneaded the tensed contours of his back. The surging rhythm of his muscles caught her senses as the flash fire between them flared out of control.

Again and again she cried out her need for him and heard his voice in her ear bearing the same message. Fierce groans tore through his body to echo the deep moans of her own desire.

Lost in a universe of limitless sensation and demanding passion, Desiree clung to her partner in the uncharted vastness with all her will. Desperately she held him to her, protectively, commandingly. For this moment in time he was hers alone and she was his. Finally, inevitably, together they reached the limit in a burst of heat that seared their skin. Then it was over. A fine mist glistened across their heated flesh, dousing the devouring flames, leaving only glowing embers of spent passion.

Desiree came slowly back to reality, aware first of the feel of Zackery's limbs tangled with hers as they lay fused together.

"I'm glad I decided to listen to you," she murmured

lazily. She rubbed her leg languidly along his until he stopped the teasing caress with a well-placed ankle.

"So am I," he agreed complacently. He raised himself on one elbow. Brushing her disordered curls back from her face with a gentle hand, his lips twisted in a curious smile. "I don't suppose you'd like to tell me why," he invited.

Desiree chuckled at his determination to fathom her reasons. "If you must know, I decided there was absolutely no valid reason to refuse what you were offering. I had promised myself when I came to Houston I was going to indulge my fantasies. Who better to teach me than a certain very attractive man I know," she explained with a touch of self-mocking humor. "It was worth it." She grinned up at him, her eyes sparkling with physical satisfaction and humor, expecting him to join her in her mood. He didn't—in fact, he looked anything but amused.

"Are you serious?" he demanded finally, the careful neutrality of his tone sounding strange, given the intimacy of their position.

Desiree nodded slowly, bewildered by the change. "Why not? After all, I was only giving you what you said you wanted."

"Is that what you really think?"

Desiree felt the compelling urgency in him with surprise. Wasn't this what he had been maneuvering for all along? "Yes," she whispered uncertainly. She was shaken by the intensity in every sharply defined line of his face. "What's wrong?" She voiced her puzzlement quietly, searching his eyes, his expression for a clue to the strange emotions swirling about their entwined bodies.

He stared back at her, his gaze as deeply probing as her own. Then he laughed, a harsh rumble of frustration and anger. "Would you believe I don't know." Levering himself away from her warmth, he sat up. "Get dressed," he grated. "I'm taking you back to the hotel."

"Now?" she demanded incredulously, unable to believe the words he tossed at her as she watched him throw on his clothes. Then, before her dazed eyes, he picked up her gown and bikini briefs and flung them across her sprawled body.

"I mean it, Desiree. If you don't get moving, I'll dress you myself."

Suddenly Desiree was hit by an all-consuming anger unlike any she had ever known. How dare this male think he could share her passion and then pack her off home like some casual fling? She might not want a commitment, but she wasn't a cheap one-night stand, either.

Grabbing her dress in one tightly clenched fist, she slid off the bed, her eyes sparking gold with the anger. "Just who do you think you are?" she growled with all the ferocity of a lioness at bay. "I will not put my clothes on"—she hurled the champagne silk bundle at the brown pelt on the bed—"and I won't leave until you give me some kind of an explanation. And that doesn't include 'I don't know,' either." She planted her hands on her hips and glared at him, completely ignoring the fact she hadn't a stitch on.

Startled by her attack, Zackery was as speechless as Desiree had been moments before. He mechanically finished tucking in his shirt, his gaze locked on Desiree's outraged face. The silence stretching between them was a living, breathing thing charged with doubt, questions, emotions, passions spent and those as yet untouched.

"I can't give you an answer, Desiree." The sincerity in Zackery's careful answer was unquestionable.

"Why not? What's so hard about telling me what's going on in your mind?"

He took a step toward her, narrowing the gap separating them to inches. He reached out his hand until his fingers brushed the stubborn fringe of curls clinging to her forehead. "All right, maybe you're right. Perhaps we'd better talk."

Steeling herself against the trembling weakness attacking her limbs at his tender gesture, Desiree forced her body to ignore its instincts. "I'm listening," she prompted on a slightly less belligerent note.

Zackery fingered the silver brown tendril he held, seemingly engrossed in the unusual shadings. "I know I've spent the entire week trying to get you into my bed. You'd think I'd be pleased at having achieved my goal, especially in view of your own attitude." He lifted his eyes to hers, allowing her to see the full scope of his own uncertainty. "But the truth is, I'm not. Hearing you explain away what we'd just shared like I've always done in the past . . ." He hesitated, obviously groping for words. "Damn it, it wasn't like that at all for me," he exploded finally.

Desiree was genuinely puzzled. "I don't know what to say," she murmured, feeling completely out of her depth.

She had been so sure Zackery had intended a lighthearted fling that she hadn't even considered the possibility that his emotions were involved. If she had, she'd never have permitted herself to get close to him. She wanted no emotional commitments, no matter how limited. After her experiences with Jeremy and her parents, she even doubted her capabilities to give love to anyone. Whatever else she might be, she wasn't a taker, nor would she ever hurt another intentionally.

"If only I'd understood." Contrition showed plainly in her eyes. She eased away from Zackery's touch to reach for her gown. "I'll be ready to leave in a moment," she offered quietly.

Zackery's hand on her shoulder halted her. "No, don't go. Stay with me tonight."

Desiree shook her head. "I can't. I misunderstood before, Zackery, but not anymore." She lifted her face, making no effort to guard her expression of regret. "A little while ago, I gave you all there was in me to give anyone. I've never done that before." She paused, shocked at the words she'd uttered without thought. She spread her hands helplessly, knowing she had to finish what she'd started. "I've been involved emotionally only once in my life and it was a disaster. I don't love well. I'm not sure I ever knew how." She stumbled over her final admission, one she had never consciously made before to anyone, even herself.

"Let me go back to my own lifestyle. I came to Houston because of Dream Magic. I meant this to be a space out of time for me, a place to play out my fantasies. When it's done, I'll return to my home and the security I've created in Atlanta."

Zackery curved both hands around her bare shoulders. "Are you sure you'll be able to go back? The woman who gave as freely as you did tonight isn't going to be satisfied with the passionless existence you just described. In fact, I don't believe she ever was, otherwise those fantasies you have would never have been born."

"Perhaps," Desiree agreed with a faint shrug. "But that doesn't change anything."

Zackery released her slowly, his fingers lingering for a moment on her golden skin. "We'll see." He turned and headed for the door. "I'll wait for you in the living room."

A little over an hour later, Desiree lay staring up at the ceiling in her darkened hotel bedroom, piecing together the events leading up to this incredible evening. Houston had certainly thrown her some surprises. From the moment of the sale of Dream Magic her life had changed out of all recognition. She had done things, said things she had never considered possible. And felt . . . too much—anger, passion, joy and sheer unadulterated desire.

For years she had lived as she had wanted. She had walked her own path in the face of parental opposition when she was younger as well as their blatant disapproval later. Except for her marriage, she had shared her life with no one on any but the most superficial of levels. With Jeremy, she had thought she'd found someone to love and be loved by. She'd been prepared to allow him to get close to her, but he hadn't wanted any part of what she offered. He'd been satisfied with surface emotions just like her family. And, like her parents, Jeremy had worshipped at the altar of the mighty god of success.

Now there was Zackery. Another one of those who forged a niche for himself in the marketplace, but with a difference. Zackery wanted more of her than she was prepared to give. How much more she wasn't certain . . . and apparently neither was he. What had started as a simple problem was now a complicated tangle.

Twisting restlessly in her bed, she thumped her pillow in self-disgust. Why hadn't she followed her first instincts and kept her distance? she chided herself. If she had, none of this would have happened. But no, she couldn't resist the allure of living out her fantasies, nor could she deny the awareness she had of Zackery, the man.

"Now what am I going to do?" she groaned aloud in frustration. "How do I get out of this situation with any kind of finesse?" She flopped over on her stomach, yanking the sheets around her bare shoulders. She glared at the illuminated face of her clock and punched her pillow again with one clenched fist. "Damn. What am I worried about anyway? I can always say no!"

Sighing in relief at the seemingly simple solution, Desiree shut her eyes firmly and willed her tense body to relax.

"Annoying man," she mumbled, beginning to drift off. "I probably won't have another fantasy tonight either. Dream Magic is going to end up Nightmare's Nightwear if I don't do . . . some . . ."

The next morning found Desiree staring resignedly at her empty sketch pad. "I wish I had never thought of this line," she muttered, her eyes narrowing with irritation. "Blast Houston and blast Zackery Taylor Maxwell and his stupid contract." Tossing her blank tablet onto her rumpled bed, she rose and padded to the bathroom.

"Maybe a hot shower will help unscramble my brains." With a quick twist of her wrist, the stall filled with steam. Shedding her ice blue lace teddy, she stepped into the heated cascade, allowing the tiny needles of warmth to soothe away the remnants of another restless night and a creatively unproductive morning. She had just finished lathering her body with her favorite jasmine soap when she became aware of a series of muted thuds coming from the sitting room.

"Naturally it's the door. What else!" she grumbled,

rinsing quickly. The second impatient summons sounded as she stepped from the shower. "All right, I'm coming." Grabbing her dusty rose velour robe, her one and only serviceable piece of at-home clothing, she whipped it around her still-damp figure and marched through her suite, ready and more than willing to do battle with the idiot banging on her door at seven-thirty on a Saturday morning. She flung it open, her tawny green gaze alive with golden flames of temper.

The sight of a mass of multicolored roses in a huge wicker basket filling the aperture stilled her angry words before they were born. The sweet floral scent embraced her as she stood staring at the glorious rainbow of blossoms.

"I come in peace." Zackery's deep drawl filtered through the wall of flowers, the teasing inflection of his voice drawing an involuntary smile from Desiree.

"At this hour," she returned, feeling some of her anger fade. The roses slowly lowered.

"You don't know how hard it was to get these," he complained mildly, his dark eyes gleaming with humor and masculine appreciation of the picture she made. "Do you know you're a little damp around the edges?"

Glancing down at the betraying splotches of moisture outlining the front of her robe, Desiree flushed slightly. "Don't just stand there. Come in before someone passes and sees me like this," she ordered, stepping back so he could enter.

Closing the door firmly behind him, Desiree surveyed her visitor and his gift. "Just what am I going to do with all those flowers? It's going to take at least a half-dozen vases to hold them."

Zackery lowered his burden onto the sofa. "Probably," he agreed, unconcerned.

He turned coffee-rich eyes to sweep the length of her figure before coming to rest on her glinting gold and emerald eyes. Something stirred in his expression, a flash of remembrance of the night before. He smiled. The lazy twist of his lips triggered all Desiree's senses. A red danger sign flared to life in her mind. Wary, uncertain of this new mood, she pulled her aloofness about her like a cloak.

"Why are you here?" she questioned carefully.

"I came to take you to breakfast."

"I can't, I'm sorry." Her response was immediate, her apology given with no real meaning. "I still need to find an apartment," she added, reinforcing her refusal.

Zackery's smile widened, although he made no move to close the gap between them. "I had a feeling you might say that, so I've been on the phone, hunting you a place to live. We have an appointment at nine-thirty to see it."

"You found me an apartment? Where?" she queried suspiciously.

"About two blocks from my place."

"Why?"

Zackery held out his hands, palms up. His eyes laughed at her wariness. "There are no hidden strings to my offer. From what you said last night, I know living here is disrupting your creative flow. Since we are business partners, I felt it would be intelligent to help you get settled," he explained reasonably.

The mention of their date gave Desiree the opening she needed to clear the air between them. "About last night," she began determinedly. "I think we should straighten out a few things if we're going to work together." She searched his face carefully for a hint to his mood. She saw no change in his faintly amused expression or his casual stance.

"Go on," he prodded.

"I want to know what you have in mind because I can tell you right now if it's more of what happened after dinner, I won't have any part of it," she stated decisively.

"You mean you won't sleep with me again?" he clarified coolly, one dark brow arched interrogatively.

"No," Desiree snapped, irritated anew at his blunt summation. Damn businessmen and their habit of cutting straight to the heart of things. A little subtlety would have been nice about now.

"I don't know what game you're playing at and I don't want to know. Last night was a mistake I don't intend repeating. As you pointed out, we're business associates, so let's just keep it that way." Desiree stared at him defiantly, every taut line of her body conveying her determination to challenge his pursuit of her.

"Okay," he agreed easily, glancing at the thin gold watch on his bronzed wrist. "You'd better get dressed if you want any breakfast."

"What?" she managed, taken aback by his easy capitulation. She eyed him in confusion. "If you think I'm going to let you find me an apartment—"

"This is business, remember," he reminded her with deceptive innocence. An innocence that was only a partial cloak for the underlying steel in his voice. "You need a place to create. Why should you object if I help you find one? After all, I'm not offering to pay the rent."

"Zackery . . ." Desiree warned, a growing conviction she was being maneuvered again nudging her consciousness.

"Desiree," Zackery retaliated. A slow sensuous drawl measured the steps he took toward her. "Have you changed your mind again?"

With a murderous glare promising future retribution, Desiree turned on her heel and stalked into her bedroom, slamming the door furiously behind her.

At first she was so angry she hardly noticed her own actions. It was only when she sat down in front of the mirror to put on her makeup that she suddenly realized the inflammatory depth of her emotions. Staring at her fiery-eyed reflection, she made an effort to control her temper.

She would not lose her cool again. She slowly smoothed on her moisturizer and blusher. She would not let Zackery goad her anymore. She brushed on incandescent emerald eye shadow to complement the pale green wrap dress she had chosen. She would make very sure her boss stuck to the letter of their contract agreement, she vowed, putting on her favorite bronze lipstick.

Deciding against taking the time to subdue her tangled mane, she settled for a quick brushing and then clipped the shiny cloud in place with two green enameled clasps behind her ears. Taking a deep, calming breath, she studied her image, checking to make sure that all signs of her internal storm were either disguised or gone. She nodded, satisfied with what she saw. She was back to normal. Veiling her eyes behind their protective screen of thick lashes, she strolled leisurely into the sitting room.

She stopped just over the threshold. Her gaze widened at the sight of vases, vases and more vases scattered about the room. Red roses, pink, yellow, white bloomed in every available space, filling the suite with their rich scent.

Smiling at her stunned reaction, Zackery moved toward her, a tiny bud vase holding one perfect yellow rose cradled in his hand. "I thought you would prefer them to stay out here, so I had the maid fix this for you." He extended his gift to her.

Caught by the extravagance of his apology and the simplicity of the single flower, Desiree's composure melted, leaving behind the warmth which was becoming a familiar companion in her previously emotionally cool existence. How could she shield herself against a man like this? she wondered as she accepted the crystal vase from him. Her instincts told her he hadn't given up—but was only biding his time, waiting for an opportunity to breach her defenses. She was fast coming to the realization that he was a worthy opponent and one, she suspected, with more skill than she had ever faced.

7

><><><><><><><><><

How big did you say this apartment was?" Desiree asked as they entered a huge modern building stretching endlessly toward the Texas sky.

"Two bedrooms, two baths."

The firm pressure on her elbow guided her toward a cleverly recessed alcove concealing a trio of elevators. "You certainly know your way around," she probed curiously as the doors slid open.

Zackery grinned down at her before punching the eighth-floor button. "A friend of mine lives here," he explained briefly.

Male or female? The swift unbidden thought flashed across Desiree's mind, dispelling some of the easy companionable feeling that had developed over breakfast. She glanced at Zackery's profile, wishing she had never allowed him to bully her into this. But had he really bullied her? Or had she simply allowed herself to accept his invitation and help under the guise of giving way to his dynamic charm?

Desiree had little time to ponder this new unsettling possibility before Zackery was ushering her inside the apartment they had come to see. It took a moment for Desiree to focus on the decor. Expecting an ordinary, well-appointed unit, Desiree was faced with an exquisitely modernized version of a regency buck's bachelor establishment.

From the terraced-foyer level, three steps curved down to acres of cream shag carpet. Cushions, overstuffed sofas and plush chairs the color of rich burgundy clustered intimately around a drawing-room-styled fireplace which dominated the main wall of the living room area. Silver and crimson blended in a wall covering that complemented the pearl-colored drapery flowing in deep swags from the windows that opened onto a stone balcony.

Why had Zackery chosen this place? she wondered, glancing at him carefully beneath the screen of her lashes. Was this a way of getting back at her for last night? She wanted to believe him incapable of such a motive, but what else could it be?

In spite of her confusion over Zackery's reasons for bringing her here, Desiree still found her innate love of color and texture responding to the room. She could feel Zackery awaiting her reaction. It was an effort to keep her expression clear of the turmoil of her thoughts. Until she knew what Zackery intended, she would keep her poise.

"Shall we start with the kitchen area first?" she suggested coolly.

Nodding with seemingly casual interest, he gestured for her to precede him down the stairs. "It's this way, I believe." He directed her to the right with a light touch on her arm.

Desiree knew he was weighing her reaction as she circled the opulent dining area, her fingers trailing pleasurably across the satin-smooth finish of the highly polished table.

Under any other circumstance, Desiree would have been delighted with the place Zackery had found for her. But not now, not like this. Not when she suspected she was the main character in an object lesson on her professed lifestyle. How dare he criticize her when he had admitted his attitude usually matched hers! He was probably wondering about her lack of comment.

"Is there a bedroom lurking about to complete this?" She gestured graphically around the room.

Puzzlement flickered briefly in Zackery's dark eyes before he nodded and indicated a hallway opposite them. "This way."

They inspected the guest room first. She noted the tastefully appointed guest suite with thinly veiled indifference. Her whole mind was locked on the door across the hall, the master bedroom. Obviously, Zackery intended to save the best for last, she observed with silent, rapidly building cynicism when she felt the intensity of his regard as he pushed open the door.

Wanting to be very sure about her suspicions, Desiree ignored Zackery for the moment and allowed her eyes to wander slowly around the room. They came to a screeching halt at the sight of the extravagant canopied bed hung with crimson velvet panels and covered with a matching spread. It was a scene straight out of a regency England love bower, complete with a satin chaise of tiny gray and red stripes positioned in front of an entire wall of delicate silver-veined mirrors. The creamy pile of the carpet was as thick as any animal pelt, creating a fantasy more stimulating than any dream she had ever had.

The sheer perfection of it finally lit the fuse to her temper. She felt betrayed by Zackery's use of her confidences. She wanted to claw and scratch in her anger, hurt him as he had hurt her. She turned, her eyes aflame with golden wrath.

"Do you like it?"

His question was so unexpected, especially the almost eager tone, that Desiree swallowed the raging words she had been about to wound him with.

"Like it?" she queried in disbelief. "Is that what I'm supposed to do?" She glared at him, suspicious, uncertain.

Zackery stared back at her. Bewilderment was clear in the look he gave her before he made a show of glancing around the exotic trysting place. "Strange, I thought this would appeal to you," he murmured, returning his attention to her.

Desiree clenched her hands into fists, the urge to hit out surprising her with its intensity. How could he do this, how could he play the innocent so well?

"Did you?" she taunted with dangerous softness. "Why? Because I was foolish enough to explain myself? I had hoped you'd understand. I should have known better. Businessmen like you never see emotions, dreams, fantasies. It's all cold logic and stark fact." She laughed without humor. She whirled around, needing to put some distance between them. She was appalled at her lack of control, shocked at the depth of her desire to hurt him.

Before she could make it to the door, Zackery's

hand closed around her shoulder, cutting off her escape. "Whoa right there," he commanded, the deep timbre of his voice as effective as his physical hold in stilling Desiree's instinctive reflex to struggle. He pulled her around to face him, determination to carry the scene out to the bitter end evident in every taut line of his body. "What in the devil has gotten into you, Desiree? Just what is going on in that exotic little head of yours?"

"You know damn well what's in my mind. You ought to, you planned it," she snapped, goaded by his continued act.

His fingers tightened in warning. "You aren't making one bit of sense."

"Okay, how's this: Man sees woman. Wants what he sees and angles to get it in bed. Woman holds off, then because she really has no real reason to refuse the man and the attraction he represents, she changes her mind. Man and woman get together, no commitment, no emotional ties, just good old-fashioned physical enjoyment. Everything should have been great, only man tossed a monkey wrench in the works by not being satisfied with the deal. Especially when the woman in question—me—gave a not-so-intelligent explanation of her reasons for her about-face."

A flicker of frustration at her inability to make Zackery see her viewpoint crossed her face. "I hurt your pride. I'm not so insensitive that I can't see that. But I truly thought I had apologized last night. Did you really have to find this . . . . this bachelor pad to show me how you felt last night?" Her voice trailed sadly into silence, the anger which prompted her outburst having given way to a pain she only vaguely understood.

Stunned, Zackery stood immobile, his hands curled around Desiree's upper arms. "I can't believe you thought me capable of a petty trick like that," he observed finally, his tone caught between astonishment and a strange kind of hurt.

His fingers tightened as he drew her to him, his eyes holding the deeply searching emerald of Desiree's. "It was never my intention to harm you. I thought only to give you pleasure. Last night you said you wanted this time to live out your fantasies." He glanced around the bedroom. "This place belongs to a friend who's spending an indefinite period of time in Europe. To me, it seemed to be the embodiment of the spirit of your Dream Magic sketches. I knew it was available for sublet." His earnest expression demanded her acceptance. "I wanted to give you a part of your dream," he finished simply.

Suspicious, yet unable to subdue the tiny spark of hope his obvious sincerity had fanned to life, Desiree stared at him mutely. For a full moment, indecision warred with the small flicker of faith. She wanted to believe him. The steady, unflinching look in his dark eyes slowly, inevitably dispelled her doubts. Yet with the knowledge of his truth another emotion reared its unwanted head—sheer unadulterated horror for her unfounded accusations. How could she have mistaken Zackery's motives so completely?

"I'm sorry," she whispered, a shimmer of remorse adding extra brilliance to her eyes.

"I can see that, Desiree, but why?" Zackery asked gently. "What have I done to give you such a low opinion of me?"

Desiree shook her head. "Nothing. Everything." She wriggled for release, suddenly needing some distance between them. How could she explain her cold, emotionless upbringing, or the ruthless precision of error and retaliation?

Zackery held her fast, ignoring her attempt to escape. "Out with it, whatever it is."

Realizing she had no real choice—in fact, in a way she owed it to him—Desiree broke her own cardinal rule. "Could we sit down?"

Zackery inclined his head without a word, simply taking her hand and leading her to a pair of chairs grouped close together near the terrace windows.

Once seated, Desiree stared out at the Houston skyline while she collected her thoughts. She had long since come to accept her background; any bitterness or resentment she might have had no longer existed. She accepted her family for what they were, not as her youthful idealism would have liked them to be. Yet the warmth of Zackery's hand on hers was somehow comforting and encouraging at the same time. Oddly, she felt in need of both feelings at the moment.

"I'm an only child of two people who really never should have had kids. I've spent my entire life in boarding schools or under the kindly impersonal supervision of various hired help. My parents were business people, successful, brilliant and very ambitious for themselves and each other. They were never cruel or intentionally neglectful. In fact, they were just the opposite in a weird sort of way. They wanted me to be like them. I had the mind, but I didn't have the killer instinct. All I ever wanted to do was design clothes. Finally, after a great deal of stubbornness on my part and disapproval on theirs, I went to college to perfect my talent. There I met a man I thought I could love. For once, my family was pleased because he was someone like themselves, someone they could understand. They were right—only I didn't realize it until it was too late. It was a disaster, so I got out, promising myself to avoid emotional involvements in the future. And I have."

She turned, meeting Zackery's eyes fully for the first time since she began her recital. "I've been taught too well to look for the self-serving motive behind any seeming kindness. It's a well-known trait in the marketplace. It means survival." She smiled crookedly. "What's been happening between us has been out of control from the first. Nothing is the way it should be and I can't handle it."

"Are you saying you're afraid of me?"

"Yes. I'm also scared of myself. You make me feel like . . ." she hesitated, momentarily at a loss.

"How do I make you feel?" he prompted softly, leaning forward in his chair. He lifted his hand to encircle her throat, his thumb on one side, while his fingers splayed possessively against the other.

The tip of Desiree's tongue danced lightly across the edge of her lower lip, moistening the slightly parched curve before she answered. Zackery's eyes followed the tiny, provocative movement as his thumb stroked gently back and forth over her jaw line.

"You took me to a place I've never been before, showed me a rainbow I've only dreamed of," she whispered honestly. "But what I said still holds true. No matter how special or rare last night was, it can't happen again. You want more of me than I'm prepared to give. To allow the attraction between us to grow will only mean pain for you and me. I won't be responsible for that."

"You think you have a choice?" The deep throbbing question beckoned her senses, recalling the images of their union, the feel of Zackery's skin against hers, the taste of his breath on her lips, the musky odor of his arousal. He rose, drawing her slowly to her feet.

Desiree swayed toward him, her body curving into his muscled length, the softness of her slender figure embracing the firmness of his. "I know I must. My body may cry out for what we create, but my mind won't be changed. There's nothing in me to give you or anyone else, Zackery. I know. I've tried and failed every time. Whatever passion I have is physical. It goes no deeper."

"We can make it if we want to badly enough," he argued, his mouth descending to hover a breath away from her lips.

"No," Desiree denied, fighting the full force of his will and the temptation he offered. "It would only be a counterfeit emotion and I won't lie either to you or myself. It's impossible to create what doesn't exist. Even fantasies have some basis to cling to, no matter how small."

"And if I want to take the chance?" His tongue flickered out to tease the fullness of her lips. "Will you risk yourself to me?"

Desiree's breath feathered unevenly over the moistened outline, setting in motion a tingling sensation which spread over her skin, rippling under the caressing stroking of his fingers on her neck. "Why?" she asked, desperately holding onto her resolve.

"For this!" His reply released the last restraint. His mouth covered hers, demanding, coaxing, ravaging, pleading in turn. An assault no defense could withstand. His tongue sipped the honey-rich essense of her. The rough rasp of the velvet rapier dueled with the pink softness of her, probing, searching for every elusive secret she would hide.

With a moan of tormented pleasure, Desiree's determination struggled briefly, then dissolved into a trembling, smoldering flame of need. Once again she was caught by the special allure Zackery had for her. Wrapping her arms around his shoulders, she molded her body to his, weaving her own spell of enchantment.

When Zackery's lips released hers, she tried one last time to stop the ravagement of her will. "Please, Zackery, don't make me hurt you. I don't want—"

"Hush," he commanded, his voice a harsh rumble against the wild pulse at the base of her throat. "I won't let you harm yourself or me. I promise."

"You can't be sure . . ." she began on a soft demented wail, clinging desperately to the fast fading reality of her decision.

"I'm certain. Trust me."

Her objection drowned in the depths of his mouth as he sought her lips once more. Following the relentless pressure of his weight against her slighter figure, Desiree backed up a pace until her legs touched the edge of the canopied bed. One more push and she sank onto the crimson softness in a controlled fall with Zackery absorbing the brunt of their combined descent.

"This is insane." Desiree sighed in surrender. "But I want to believe you." Her eyes sought his, wonder obscuring the passion for a moment. "How did that happen?"

Zackery grinned wickedly. "Does it really matter right now?" he asked, his hands finding the tie at her waist which held her dress in place.

She shook her head wordlessly, her lashes fanning her cheeks beneath the flaming want in his dark gaze. No, it really was unimportant to them at this moment. The chemistry between them, the fire consuming her, blotted out rational thinking. The touch of Zackery's sure hands on her lace-cupped breasts made her quiver with barely contained desire. Her fingers sought the buttons of his shirt in an instinctive need to feel his bare skin once more. As she pushed the fabric down his shoulders, her bra slithered away beneath his deft manipulations. In a matter of seconds, her pale green bikini briefs vanished. Tracing languid, teasing little circles along the length of her leg from ankle to thigh, his caresses flowed over her trembling body. Ripple after ripple feathered her tingling skin until she moaned softly.

Apparently satisfied with his efforts, Zackery pulled away for a moment, sliding quickly, impatiently out of his remaining clothes and returning to her welcoming arms with a hoarse whisper of his own urgent need. He gathered her close, burying his lips in the curve of her shoulder. Nipping gently, his hand closed possessively over her breast. The firming nipple beneath his palm drew a low groan of masculine triumph as his lips captured the rosy bud.

"It's not supposed to be like this," Desiree breathed, her hands searching and finding the most sensitive pleasure points of her man.

"No?" Zackery mocked indulgently. He raked a trail of pulsing sensation across the other taut nipple, down her sensitive stomach and along her thigh with his hand, then retraced it with his lips.

Desiree twisted her fingers passionately in his hair as he slid down her quivering body. When his daring, demanding kisses found the center core of her passion, she cried out.

"Oh Zackery. You're driving me out of my mind. I'm on fire. . . ."

He turned his head to brand the inside of each of her thighs with the searing moistness of his tongue. Desiree shifted reflexively, allowing him the total freedom of the territory he had claimed.

"So am I," he murmured thickly, his fingers cradling her curving bottom. "Last night was only an appetizer. There's so much more for us. . . ."

"You're so certain," Desiree purred, writhing under his caresses. Her breaths came in tiny quick pants, a primitive rhythm indicating the depth of her raging hunger.

"Soon you will be, too," he vowed as he raised himself over her.

The smoldering fire in his eyes matched the molten jade of Desiree's own. Zackery's hard, taut body covered her, filling her, possessing her, making her his chosen mate.

Lured and seduced by his raw power, Desiree clung to him, drawing him into her spell. She'd have all of him—every thought, every need, every desire. He was hers, on this level irretrievably, undeniably hers. Just as he had been last night.

"I want you, my Zackery," she commanded, staking her claim to him with her words and the arching, pleading contortions of her aroused body.

Responding to her cries, he moved against her with teasing, provoking strokes designed to withhold the ultimate union for a little longer. "No more denials?" he murmured huskily, a yearning lacing the fierce throb of his voice.

"No," Desiree confessed raggedly, her head thrown back against the deep crimson spread. "I want you too much to deny anything." The shattering truth burst upon her consciousness, searing her mind. Never had she wanted, needed anything or anyone as she did Zackery. Never had she known this compulsion to possess and be possessed.

"I knew you would give me the words we needed," he swore. His hands tightened on her shoulders, chaining her to their pallet as he surged passionately against her. Desiree surrounded the hard, urgent probe of his body, sheathing it with her strength, drawing it to the very center of her being.

Zackery crushed her until they seemed to merge into one entity, a shimmering, glistening creature arching, undulating, swirling in a sensual dance of wild untamed desire.

"My God, woman," Zackery groaned, licking the salty beads of perspiration which lay like jewels upon the curve of her breast.

Desiree had no words with which to answer. Zackery had tapped her deepest sensuality, made her aware of her femininity as never before. He awoke a primitive side of her nature she'd had no knowledge of—and she was caught in its ruthless yet tender grip. Civilization and all her sophistication were like smoke in the wind.

Burying her face against his damp chest, she inhaled the earthy scent of his arousal. The thrust of him carried them onward, closer and closer to the heights just ahead. Suddenly she was poised there, trembling, burning, aching—

A final deep surge lifted them together up and over. . . .

"Zackery!" The cry of triumph arched her throat, tautening every sinew.

"Desiree!" Zackery's muffled shout of satisfaction followed her as they spiraled down . . . down . . . down into the soft warmth of fulfillment.

Silence wrapped around them as they lay together. Late morning sunlight played across their gleaming bodies, bathing them in a soft golden glow. With a sigh, Zackery rolled onto his side, his fingers curled possessively around Desiree's breast.

"Are you sorry?" he questioned quietly, his eyes demanding her honesty.

"No," Desiree replied, lifting her hand to the side of his face to follow the sharp path of his jaw line. "If I had a wish, it would be that my nature were different than it is."

"Are you really so sure it isn't?" Zackery answered whimsically.

Desiree turned on her side, lifting her gaze to meet the surprisingly vulnerable expression of his own.

"I don't know anymore," she offered slowly, seriously. "Since coming here, I feel like someone I hardly recognize. I meant this time as an amusing game, a masquerade in a sense. But always in the back of my mind, I knew it to be a fantasy . . . yet it seems so real."

Zackery smiled gently as he used his thumb to soothe away the lines of confusion marking her forehead. "Thank you for that, little cat. I know what it cost you to admit it. Will you do one more thing for me . . . for us?"

Desiree eyed him warily, not liking the careful neutrality of his tone nor the waiting stillness of his body. "What?" she prompted gravely, wondering what was coming.

"Will you allow our relationship to happen? Will you let it grow without trying to control or stifle it?"

Desiree sucked in her breath on a soft gasp at the all-encompassing concession. It was tantamount to surrender. "An affair," she clarified.

"If that's all you'll give me," he agreed, watching her intently.

"Will you be satisfied with that?"

He shrugged dismissively. "I'll have to be if it's all I can get."

Desiree studied him silently, wanting to question him further yet strangely wary of what he might say. She sensed there was an elusive something hovering on the edges of recognition. Promising, enticing, an unknown waiting to be discovered.

"Will you give me that much, Desiree? Will you share the fire with me?"

Unable to deny the deep desire within, the challenge of the passion he offered, Desiree smiled wickedly, feeling a sudden surge of anticipation for what lay ahead. "I'll grant you your fantasy," she decreed solemnly, her golden emerald eyes dancing with teasing lights.

"Okay, vixen, my dream it is." He half grinned, lifting a hand to ruffle her already tangled hair. "Come on," he ordered, giving her hip a gentle tap. "Let's get moving. We've got to sign the papers for the sublet, get your clothes from the hotel and check out, shop for food—"

"Enough," Desiree interrupted with a groan. "I'm not going to do all that today."

"Yes, you are," Zackery countered ruthlessly, tossing her dress to her. "I'll even take you out to dinner as a reward if you get that gorgeous body of yours in motion—Texas motion, I mean, not Georgia slow."

"That's not fair," Desiree complained lightly, beginning to dress. "I'm not that slow."

"Honey, don't tell lies." Zackery leaned across to cover her mouth briefly with the warmth of his lips. "One of the things I . . . like about you best is your easy way of speaking, and the way you glide instead of walking like the rest of us humans."

Desiree heard the slight hesitation in Zackery's comment, but ignored it as unimportant, being more intrigued by his word-picture of her. "Am I really like that?"

He nodded emphatically while he tucked his shirt into his slacks. He indicated her half-dressed state. "I'm done and guess what?"

"I'm not," she finished for him, slipping her arms into her dress and pulling it around her slender figure. "I'm certainly not going to race around in your wake," she muttered as she fumbled her way into her heels.

"We'll see." Zackery chuckled affectionately. He waited patiently while Desiree ran a brush through her hair and resecured the clasps holding her tumbled mane in place.

"Ready?"

"No, but I don't think it matters, does it?" Desiree retorted tartly. "In fact, I'm beginning to think—"

Zackery touched her lips with his forefinger, stilling her words. "No thinking allowed. Not today. Will you let me do the planning for us?"

Desiree stared at him, caught by the undisguised plea in his voice. For a moment she was torn between the habits of years of self-sufficiency and a surprisingly strong desire to grant Zackery's request. One part of her had no wish to give up the smallest piece of her independence, yet another, until recently undiscovered side of her nature welcomed the idea of someone to lean on, if only for a short, not to be repeated, heartbeat.

"All right," she agreed softly. The instant warmth kindled in Zackery's rich coffee eyes startled her. She withdrew into flippancy as a shield against the emotions she neither wanted to feel nor was prepared to face. "You may do all the thinking, just as long as I don't need to tackle that horrendous list you've got in mind."

Ignoring her rider, Zackery took her arm, tucking it under his. He smiled down into her slumberous eyes. "You know, you remind me of a grumpy lioness when you try to put me in my place," he remarked, escorting her from the apartment.

"Watch that you don't get clawed," Desiree quipped with all the deceptive innocence of the cat he named her.

"I think I can handle a little mauling if the prize is great enough."

The sheer masculine assurance of the gently spoken statement reminded Desiree of her vulnerability where this man was concerned. Not that she needed any hints, she observed in silent denunciation. After all, hadn't she just agreed to a relationship in spite of her intentions to keep Zackery at a safe distance? Hadn't she succumbed to his physical allure when she had promised herself she wouldn't? And now, hadn't she given him the rights to her decisions for a day? Small things, each one, yet together they represented a wide breach in her protective shell. Where was she headed? Where was Zackery leading her . . . them? And more importantly, why was she allowing it to happen? Because of a fantasy? A wish for memories? A desire for . . . Her mind balked at completing her trend of thought.

"First the realtors," Zackery suggested, opening the door for Desiree. "Then we'll stop by the hotel for your clothes. After that, lunch."

"Slavedriver," Desiree responded in a deliberate attempt to subdue the torrent of questions flooding her mind. The last thing she needed was to let Zackery see the turmoil raging within. She had a feeling she had already betrayed herself quite enough.

8

Ooh, that's the best my poor feet have felt all afternoon." Desiree sighed wearily, easing her over-worked toes from her strappy heels. After wriggling the offended digits experimentally, she curled her legs under her and nestled into the cushiony softness of Zackery's sofa.

"It wasn't that bad." Zackery crossed the room bearing a drink in each hand. "Your wine." He handed her the slender fluted glass of pale liquid before taking his place beside her.

Desiree sipped appreciatively. "You weren't the one tramping around in these shoes," she retaliated, glancing meanfully at Zackery's comfortable footwear.

"I told you to change those spindly things," he pointed out self-righteously. Positioning himself comfortably in the angle of the couch arm, he carefully pulled Desiree over to lean against him, supporting her in turn with his body.

Relaxing against him, she wiggled a bit to find just the right spot.

"Now drink your wine and listen to the music," he drawled in her ear as he laid the side of his cheek against her temple. "We've had a long day and a good dinner, thanks to Vanderbilt, so let's enjoy the peace for a while. Then I'll take you home, I promise."

Lulled by the soothing melody in the background and Zackery's warmth surrounding her, Desiree accepted his assurance he would let her go home to her own bed. Why he was giving her this breathing space seemed unimportant compared to the pleasure of simply being held.

Zackery made no demands; he just cradled her in his arms as though he simply enjoyed being next to her. Desiree drifted deeper into the languid drowsiness preceding sleep. The tension, the wariness, her careful guard—all gradually floated away. Her eyelids grew heavy until it was easier to let them drift shut than struggle to hold them open. The slow, steady beat of Zackery's heart beneath her ear assumed a low, soothing hypnotic rhythm carrying her closer to sleep. Her hand relaxed its grip on her empty glass. The soft thud of the fragile crystal against the plush pile of the carpet disturbed her and her lashes fluttered briefly.

"Wake up, sleepyhead," Zackery shook her gently awake.

"No, this is much too cozy," she mumbled, trying to burrow into his chest again. "I'm . . ."

Zackery held her pliant body away from him. "Do you really mean what you're saying? Do you want to stay the night here . . . with me?" he demanded, his words distinctly spaced in an effort to reach her.

Zackery's offer shattered the magic intimacy of their closeness, recalling Desiree to reality. "No." She struggled through the mists of sleep clouding her mind. "No," she repeated more clearly as her eyes opened and she drew herself away from the seductive, tempting haven of his touch.

Zackery's lips twisted ruefully. "Somehow I had a feeling you'd say that." He sighed deeply, stretched, then got to his feet. He extended his hand. "Let's go before I change my mind," he suggested in a tone which conveyed the restraint he was exercising in keeping his promise.

Amazed at the hunger reflected clearly in his dark gaze, Desiree found her own willpower wavering. There was something incredibly persuasive about a man of Zackery's undeniable sexuality wanting her— not just as a soft body in his bed, but as a thinking, feeling woman. He had shown her often enough he desired her physically, yet tonight he had also demonstrated his care of her as a person. He had been surprisingly sensitive to her obvious weariness and her need to have some time alone.

The short drive back to her new apartment was completed in relative silence with Zackery leaving her at her door with a brief hard kiss and an equally short goodnight. Moments later, Desiree tumbled tiredly into bed, the firm pressure of Zackery's lips and the clean taste of him following her into a deep, contented sleep.

Then the dream began. A lush green meadow surrounded by stately trees. Leafy branches waved gently over the downy soft spring grass. The scent of unseen flowers drifted with the light, cooling breezes, creating nature's own melody. A woman stood poised in the dark shadows at the edge of the clearing, her glowing jade eyes intent on the figure seated on a large, flat rock in the center of the small glen. Apparently unaware of being observed, the man rose, displaying a firmly muscled bronze body draped with a single rich sable pelt at his waist.

The woman took an unwary step forward, drawn by the sheer artistry and beauty of his gleaming physique. A twig crackled beneath her slender foot. She froze as the dark brown head swung unerringly in her direction, pinning her with fathomless dark eyes.

She stood transfixed as the piercing gaze swept her tousled, flower-strewn hair, down her bare shoulders to the swells of her lightly veiled breasts. The silent survey approved the semi-transparent layers of whisper-fine primrose silk which barely concealed the golden skin to a point just below her hips. Undisguised desire smoldered in his eyes as they traveled slowly down the tapering length of her long legs.

Quietly the man padded toward her, stalking her with a hunter's intent. The woman turned her head, mutely seeking shelter, safety from his careful advance. He drew near—she dodged agilely to one side—he cut her off. Closer now, the scent of his masculinity filled her nostrils as attraction and fear uncoiled within her. She sidestepped once more as caution prevailed. He was before her, halting her flight. Only a breath separated them.

He held her wary eyes with his, reading the controlled panic in their gold-shot depths. Helplessly the female gazed into the hunter's sharp-planed face, knowing escape was impossible. Fatalistically, she waited, head bowed, for his domination. It never came. Instead a husky whisper of male need called her name.

Desiree.

She looked up and found herself captured by the gentle smile curving the lips of her captor. Her eyes widened as he held out his hand to her—a silent plea for her willing surrender.

"Zackery," she whispered softly in the stillness of the early dawn hours. The sound of her own voice dispelled the dream, bringing Desiree into full wakefulness. Momentarily disoriented by the strangeness of her surroundings, Desiree lay staring into the gradually lightening gloom.

Suddenly the confusion, the indecision of the past week seemed to gather about her, focusing on her dream. It was so similar to the one she'd had in Atlanta, the one that had spawned Emerald Enchantment, it was uncanny.

The stark loneliness of her life in Atlanta was a haunting specter compared to the golden haze of Houston, she realized with brutal insight. Her dreams, her designs were only a poor substitute for the emptiness around her. She needed more, much more. She wanted, no, she needed love. To be loved and more importantly, someone to love. Zackery. His name flashed against the storm of mental searching. The clouds of doubt in her mind cleared, leaving her with one stark truth. She loved Zackery. Irretrievably, irreversibly and without a single excuse, she loved him as she had loved no one person in her life—ever.

That was why she wanted to run as far as she could, yet stay at one and the same time. It was also the reason she'd shared Zackery's bed and later drawn back, hoping to keep their relationship on a business footing. She had loved him even then—loved him for how he made her feel and the depth of emotion he touched in her.

He was the man of her fantasies. The one who had shown himself to be understanding of her complex personality. He admired her skills as a designer, he enjoyed her sense of humor and fully repaid it in kind. He allowed her the freedom to be true to her own sensuous nature, but most of all, he made her feel like a desirable, passionate woman. His woman.

Desiree slipped from the sheets and moved to the windows overlooking slumbering Houston. In many ways, she was like the city below waiting for the sunrise of a new day. She, too, had been at rest, emotionally and physically. It had taken Zackery's dynamic power to stir her to life, to create reality out of fantasy, kindle desire into love.

Whether Zackery himself loved her, she did not know. His reaction to their first night together suggested some deeper feeling than just a man's need of a woman, but that was a far cry from love. He could be intrigued by her, curious perhaps. His possessiveness could be a normal quirk of his businessman's acquiring personality.

Desiree's forehead crinkled into tiny lines of displeasure at her thoughts. She wanted more than this . . . much more. She wanted him on every level. She needed his love in ways she barely understood, since they were so new to her.

But he only wanted an affair, the voice of reason reminded her sharply. He had hinted at more, it was true. A mistress? His lady? His wife? It could be any or none. What did she want besides his love? To share his life? His name? Bear his children?

Desiree pressed her hands to her ears in a vain

attempt to shut out the endless list of questions besieging her to which there were no answers. She had only one fact to cling to—she loved Zackery. Where she was going, what he wanted from her, paled beside the awesome discovery of her own passion. For now she would accept what they had together. Her solitary nature demanded she allow Zackery the dignity of making up his mind unhindered by her. Just as she traveled alone, so must he. To do otherwise would invite a falseness which neither of them deserved.

The relief of her decision brought a sigh to her lips and a sense of calm to her chaotic thoughts. She focused on the horizon, watching with pleasure the delicate shades of color shimmering across the silver gray trail of night's end. The sun peered over the edge of the world, bringing life-giving warmth and light, dispelling the darkness. The melodic chime of her bedside phone interrupted her enjoyment of nature's spectacular ritual. Turning away, she moved leisurely to her night table.

"Watching the dawn, honey?" Zackery's deep-throated growl stroked the ear pressed against the receiver.

"Yes," she replied softly. She curled up on the edge of the bed, tucking her bare legs under her. The feather-trimmed hem of her black toga-style nightie just brushed the top of her thighs as she nestled in the stack of pillows behind her back. "I didn't know you were an early riser, too."

The rich sound of Zackery's laughter reached across the distance separating them to wrap around her like a warm embrace. "If I didn't get up at this hour, I wouldn't accomplish half of what I need to do," he commented wryly. "Which brings me to why I'm calling. I'd planned to spend the day with you, but thanks to a New York cry for help, I've got to catch a flight in a couple of hours."

Desiree nibbled at her lower lip, dismayed at the prospect of Zackery's absence. "Nothing serious, I hope?" she probed delicately.

"Bad enough," he replied, the sudden harshness of his tone conveying the gravity of the situation more eloquently than words. "In fact, the way it looks now, I'll be lucky to get back before next week. How many sketches have you finished?" he asked, changing the subject abruptly.

Desiree was silent for a moment, while she made a mental tally. "Fourteen, counting the six I submitted at the outset. Why?"

"Because I want to step up production if we can. There's been a breach in security in New York. I'm not sure yet whether it affects Dream Magic or not. I want to minimize the risk as much as possible. The sooner we get this line on the market the better."

"I only need to complete four more designs to finish out the eighteen you wanted to start," Desiree stated, doing some rapid thinking of her own. "I should be able to knock those out in a couple of days."

"Good. I've already called Jim," he explained, naming his vice-president and right-hand man. "He'll help you with the promo package. I'm giving you Marsha as well. Now, what about materials? I haven't had a chance to read Marsha's workup on that yet. We found a model, at least."

"As far as fabrics go, you had a fairly good selection to choose from in the warehouse. All but five of the fourteen are coming from there. The others will be divided between Irish lawn and oriental silk."

"And the ones you haven't finished?"

"Again the warehouse. In fact, the ideas were prompted by some swatches I saw," Desiree admitted. "When is the model arriving, or is she already here? We're going to need her measurements to get the gowns ready."

"Don't remind me. She's in New York now. As soon as I get there, I'll either have her put on a plane or get her sizes out to you. Can you think of anything we've missed?"

Desiree searched her mind, knowing the importance of the project underway and the reasons for pushing it through. Fashion espionage was no new practice. Every designer knew its power and jealously guarded his creations as zealously as any country ever watched over national secrets.

"Not right now," Desiree replied finally.

"Okay, until I get back, you're in charge of Dream Magic. I've already put Jim and Marsha in the picture. They'll help you any way they can, but yours is the final say," Zackery announced flatly.

Desiree's eyes widened in astonishment at his unlooked-for and unwelcome decree. "You can't be serious," she gasped. "I'm not qualified for this and you know it. I sure as the devil don't want it."

"I'm well aware of that, believe me," Zackery shot back. "However, what you want isn't under discussion. We've got a contract, remember. Together, we both stand to lose too much if you don't take over for me. Or would you rather take the chance on Dream Magic being put out by some other house under another name?" He paused, letting his words sink in. "Trust me, Desiree. I wouldn't ask you to do anything I didn't think you could handle," he added on a softer note. "You've got a sharp mind under that lazy exterior and we both know it. Don't be afraid to use it just because of some misguided attempt to deny your heritage. It's no crime to be successful or ambitious."

Surprised once again at his perception where she was concerned, Desiree felt herself weakening. He was right, she rationalized silently. With him gone, she was the best one—no, the only one other than Zackery—equipped to oversee the birth of her fantasy.

"All right, I'll do it," she agreed in resignation. "But I'm not—"

"Thanks, honey." Zackery's deep voice interrupted Desiree's objections before they began. "I've got to get a move on if I want to catch my flight. I'll call you in the morning about the model. See if you can work in some time to miss me while I'm gone." The last order came out in a husky growl of male need.

Desiree's eyes glowed jade with the memories the sound invoked. "Oh, I'll miss you all right," she teased softly. She smiled in satisfaction at Zackery's drawn hiss of surprise at her seductive purr. "I can't wait for you to get back"—she paused artistically—"so you can take over Dream Magic."

There was a full second of silence on the other end of the line before Zackery's rueful laughter rumbled in Desiree's ear. "If you live to grow one year older, Desiree Beaumont, it won't be because of your own efforts, I can promise that."

Desiree was still grinning at Zackery's parting shot when she hung up the phone and headed for the bath. No—shower, she amended on second thought. Employing the speed which was fast becoming typical of her since working for Zackery, Desiree completed her morning ritual and had breakfast in record time. Since Zackery had seen fit to entrust her with the bringing to life of Dream Magic, she had no intention of failing him or herself. Her lack of actual experience in heading a project of this magnitude was a decided drawback. But fortunately, she did have the knowledge of what was required and, thanks to Zackery's top-notch organization, the personnel to carry out her instructions with a minimum amount of fuss. With the help of Marsha, Z.T.'s secretary, and Jim, Taylor/Maxwell's vice-president, and herself, they should be able to handle everything until Zackery got back . . . she hoped.

Desiree arrived at Taylor/Maxwell's nearly deserted office complex. Since it was Sunday, only the security people were on the premises to notice her entrance. She rode the empty elevator up to the top floor, barely noticing her surroundings. Her mind was tuned to the remaining four sketches she needed. Fortunately, she had been turning them around in her head for a few days, so they were ready to be put on paper. That was the first order of business. She needed those designs immediately so the pattern makers could begin work on them. Without the constant interruptions which plagued regular work hours, she hoped to complete them all before the day was over.

Pausing only long enough to drop her bag, Desiree headed straight for her drawing board. Minutes ticked by as her pencil skimmed rapidly across the sheet, leaving a trail of elegant, finely defined lines of startling simplicity. Colors and minor adaptations were noted before the gown was signed, then set aside to make room for another. Desiree had just finished her second creation when a tap on her door interrupted her concentration.

"Come in," she called, straightening from her slightly bent position. She glanced over her shoulder, wondering who her visitor was.

"I brought the schedule sheet over so you could see

exactly where we are," Marsha James began without preamble. The slender brunette crossed the carpet in a few brisk strides and placed the precisely typed papers in front of Desiree.

Strangely unsurprised at the appearance of Z.T.'s secretary, Desiree gestured toward a second tall stool at the end of her raised worktable. "Have a seat while I go over these," she suggested with a faint smile of welcome. During the short time she had been at Taylor/Maxwell's she had come to like and respect Marsha. Efficient, well groomed and always in control of any situation, she was all a top management assistant should be, but with the added bonus of being surprisingly human on closer acquaintance.

"I should have brought us some coffee," Marsha commented, taking the place Desiree offered. "I'm afraid Z.T.'s call must have addled my brains."

Desiree grimaced. "Don't even think such a thing, let alone say it." She tapped a finger sharply against the sheath of work she held. "It's going to take every bit of skill you, Jim and I have got to hurry Dream Magic along."

Marsha nodded her sleek dark head in agreement. "And hopefully, some good ole-fashioned Texas gambler's luck."

"Amen!"

They eyed one another in silence, contemplating the Herculean task before them.

"Will they take orders from me?" Desiree asked finally, referring to the multitude of people needed to put her fantasy into production.

"With Zackery calling the shots, you doubt it?" Marsha's tone conveyed her surprise at Desiree's question.

Desiree's gaze met the secretary's with clear-eyed

candor. "If I had any experience in a project of this scope, or if I had some time with the company—no. However, considering the circumstances, it would be odd if someone didn't question my abilities and my meteoric rise. Even you must have some curiosity," she added, getting to the crux of the matter.

If there were suspicions in Marsha's mind, she wanted them aired here and now, before they embarked on a close working relationship. Uncertain how long Zackery would be gone, she had to be prepared to shoulder her unwilling role for an indefinite period of time. That would be more difficult, if not impossible, with one of her main sources of knowledge and help lacking confidence in her judgment.

The brunette shrugged, her expression faintly amused. "I've been with Z.T. since I graduated from school. Believe me, I *know* he wouldn't have put you in charge if he didn't have complete faith in your skills. Where work is concerned, Z.T. doesn't allow personal considerations to enter into his decisions."

Reassured, Desiree returned her companion's grin. "Good enough. Have you been in touch with Jim?"

Marsha shook her head. "No, but Z.T. had called him before he got me. His orders were to let Jim handle the promotional stuff, media coverage, advertisements and so forth. I'm to set up the preview show and line up the models to showcase our 'Dream Magic Girl.'"

"That leaves me to turn the designs into reality." Desiree scanned the complete list of her creations and their various stages of development. "From the looks of this, we've made a good start, but we'll have to work flat out if we're to get the rest of these done ahead of schedule. Our original date was cutting it fine."

"I know," Marsha agreed unhesitatingly, "but we don't really have a choice if security has been breached. One whiff of your innovative concept and every house in the country will be copying us overnight. The market will be flooded with cheap imitations quicker than you can draw a breath."

"Not if I can help it," Desiree shot back, an unexpected anger making her voice sharp with determination. Hearing Marsha bluntly put into words what they all knew was a very real possibility made her temper boil. These were her dreams, her ideas, and she'd be damned if any underhanded, conniving little fashion pirate was going to get his sneaky hands on them. She, Zackery and Taylor/Maxwell were going to get the job done if they all had to work 'round the clock to do it.

"That's why I'm here today. I wanted to get a chance to flesh out the remaining gowns. I want them ready for the pattern people first thing Monday!"

Marsha nodded briskly before sliding off her stool. "Okay, boss. While you're doing that, I'll rustle us up some coffee, then I'll get to work on phoning the department heads. It'll save us calling a meeting tomorrow and give them time to think about rescheduling possibilities." Marsha headed for the door. "Are sandwiches all right with you for lunch or do you want me to get reservations for you somewhere?" she asked, pausing on the threshold.

"Whatever you're doing is fine with me, unless you've got other plans," Desiree replied easily but with a definite purpose. She had no desire to establish herself as some power mogul taking advantage of Zackery's absence. Her work with Manuelo had been diversified in spite of Laura's not-so-kind remarks about her being a glorified gofer. But Dream Magic's promotion would stretch her to the limits and she knew it. She knew she needed Marsha's help and wasn't above admitting it openly. She was well aware that Zackery's orders demanded Marsha's cooperation, but it did not command her good will or respect. That Desiree knew she would have to earn for herself.

A faint glimmer of pleasure flickered in Marsha's blue eyes at the invitation before a grin animated her face. She scanned Desiree's sleek figure. "Sunday is my cheat day. I don't suppose you'd like pizza?" she teased hopefully.

"Love it." Desiree's prompt acceptance drew a disbelieving chuckle from the secretary. "As long as there's scads of cheese," she qualified with a slang phrase dredged up from her college days.

"Done!" Marsha agreed, setting the seal on lunch and Desiree's overture all in one stroke.

When Marsha left, Desiree turned back to her sketching table to begin work on her third drawing. The last two of her ideas were the newest and least thought out, and therefore the most difficult to reproduce. She barely nodded to Marsha when she returned a short time later with the promised coffee. She sipped the fragrant brew absently as she eyed the half-completed gown in front of her.

"I hate deadlines," she muttered beneath her breath as she carefully erased the moderately plunging scooped neckline and penciled in a daring neck-to-waist slash.

She caught her lower lip between her teeth, mentally visualizing the one-dimensional drawing in its glorious reality. Coloring the fluid chiffon in variegated shades of mint to deepest jade, she viewed the creation critically, keeping in mind the male's appreciation of a subtly veiled female form. She was still ironing out the several small details that didn't quite suit her exacting eye when Marsha appeared at her door with the flat box containing their lunch. The savory aroma of pizza seemed incongruous in the elegant surroundings of her office, but Desiree was too hungry to care.

"Where shall I put this?" Marsha asked, waving one hand carrying two sodas at the white box she held in the other.

"Anywhere except on these drawings," Desiree replied, sliding wearily off her perch. Stretching to relieve her cramped muscles, she sighed deeply. "What time is it? In all the rush to get over here this morning, I forgot to put on my watch."

"Just after two," Marsha answered, setting out the napkins and extra cheese shaker on the low table in front of the couch. "I got so darned involved with those calls, I forgot all about lunch until my stomach started rumbling." She glanced up with a rueful grimace as Desiree took her place on the sofa. "You don't suppose it's an omen, do you?" she asked half seriously.

"No way," Desiree denied with feeling. "We're going to do this."

Marsha's expression conveyed an uncharacteristic look of doubt. "Do you realize how much there is—I mean really is—left to do?" she questioned. "I've spoken to every one of our heads. I don't see how we can pull this off. They don't either."

"We can because we've got to," Desiree stated with quiet conviction.

She was startled by the calm certainty of her belief. Where had her confidence come from? A few hours ago she had been objecting strenuously to being in charge, yet here she was now not only accepting the power Zackery had given her but reassuring someone else about the job ahead. The metamorphosis was as bewildering as it was unexpected. Desiree wanted, no, needed to examine the change, yet this was neither the time nor the place. Right now Dream Magic was all that mattered.

In spite of the casual atmosphere of their meal, their conversation centered on Marsha's morning activities and the department heads' reaction to the crisis. Understandably concerned, each boss had promised to revamp schedules and personnel to meet the demand of the situation. What none of them could give, however, was his or her assurance of shaving much time off the already rushed completion date.

"I wish Zackery knew for certain whether Dream Magic has been compromised," Marsha commented wistfully. She rose and began collecting the debris from their lunch.

"Knowing Zackery, he won't leave any avenue unexplored if there's a chance to find out," Desiree replied absently, her mind already immersed in the sketch she had been working on before their break.

Marsha glanced at her, a tiny satisfied smile curving her lips. "He does have that reputation," she teased gently.

Marsha's complacent tone brought Desiree back to earth with a bump. Raising her head, she frowned at the other woman. "I thought we settled this earlier," she remarked carefully, referring to her relationship with her employer.

Her companion's grin was wicked. "Oh, I meant what I said this morning," she assured her on a stifled chuckle, "but if you're going to read Zackery's character so well, no one else will believe it's all business between you."

Desiree just managed to bite back the blistering rebuttal aching for expression when she read the kindness and understanding in Marsha's eyes. Some of her annoyance died in the face of Marsha's unquestioning attitude. "I'll need to be more careful, I guess," she offered finally, tacitly admitting to an intimacy between her and Zackery. It was inevitable that Marsha'd guess, she realized, and surprisingly, she found that she didn't really mind.

"It would be best, as you know," Marsha agreed on a more serious note. "Z.T. has a reputation." She shrugged. "A lot of people will envy you your place with him and with Taylor/Maxwell. Neither you nor Z.T. need that right now."

"I know, Marsha, but what disturbs me is how you could tell." Desiree's voice demanded an explanation.

"I've known Z.T. a long time, even before I started to work for him. I've never seen him react to a woman the way he does to you. Being in the same room with you both is like standing too close to a bonfire."

"No." Desiree groaned in dismay.

"Yes," Marsha mocked kindly. She smiled. "But don't worry. If I hadn't known Z.T. since I was a kid, I don't think I'd have noticed anything, and you're as accomplished at hiding your feelings as he is."

"Dutch comfort?"

Marsha collected the last of the leftovers into a tidy bundle. "It's better than nothing."

Desiree grimaced. "Thanks a lot. I think I'd rather get back to work than continue this questionable line of conversation."

Marsha laughed aloud. "You're even beginning to sound like our esteemed employer," she teased before she sauntered out the door, her amusement trailing behind her to taunt Desiree at odd moments during the remainder of the afternoon.

By sheer force of will, Desiree managed to complete the third sketch to her satisfaction and begin the fourth. She was still struggling with the final touches when Marsha left at five. It was early evening before Desiree locked away the finished sketches and headed back to her apartment.

Weary from the intense concentration of her day, she shed her clothes and treated her exhausted body to a long, relaxing soak in a warm tub. As she unwound from the worries Zackery had piled on her shoulders, she found her mind drifting back to the passion they had shared.

The silken caress of the scented water against her skin echoed the sensitivity of Zackery's touch. The heat of her bath was a faithful reminder of the searing intensity of the pleasure he created out of his desire for her. Sighing in the lonely splendor of her aquatic environment, Desiree surrendered to the deep, aching need Zackery's absence had brought to her self-contained life. She hadn't wanted Zackery in spite of the instantaneous attraction. She had meant to keep her freedom, her unencumbered state of oneness, yet she had not been able to resist the sheer, unsheathed power of Zackery's appeal. Even her hatred of the business world, its questionable ethics and cold-blooded approach, had fallen beneath Zackery's lethal spell.

The white-hot fires of desire had burned into her very soul, destroying the barriers that guarded her heart. Out of the devastation of her defenses, love had risen like a phoenix from the ashes of its pyre. Spreading its wings, it had soared, unfettered, wild and free to ride the fierce winds of passion and desire, reaching ever higher to the sun. Zackery was her sun, the blinding splash of life-giving energy warming the cool, empty vastness of her life with love and a purpose for existing.

Smiling wistfully at the poetic tribute her thoughts had conjured up, Desiree brought her mind back to reality. She had to quit fantasizing about her relationship with Zackery. The desire he had for her gave her no rights other than to share his bed. She couldn't force his love and she wouldn't, even if she had the power. She wanted him only if he could come to her freely. If he came . . .

The soft ring of the bedroom extension interrupted Desiree's musings. With a muttered oath, she rose from her bath and whipped the burgundy bath sheet around her dripping form. Zackery! The name blazed across her consciousness. He had called just as he promised. A confusion of emotion suffused her being, bringing a faint flush of pink to her golden skin. Hurrying through the connecting door, she dashed for the phone beside her bed. She was slightly breathless as she murmured a greeting into the receiver.

"Where the devil have you been?" Zackery all but roared in her ear without bothering to say hello.

9

~~~~~~~~~~~

At work," Desiree was startled into answering. Dumbfounded at the angry male tirade, her pleased anticipation ebbed away.

"On Sunday?" The outright skepticism of Zackery's reply conveyed his disbelief all too effectively.

A slow burning annoyance cooled Desiree's voice and tightened her muscles. "Yes, on Sunday," she confirmed in her most languid drawl. "I mistakenly thought you'd be pleased since I managed to finish the last sketches we needed to fill out Dream Magic." The biting sarcasm of her retort brought a strange silence to the other end of the line.

Desiree gripped the receiver hard in an effort to control her mounting temper. Blast him. He'd done it again! Once more he'd forced her into defending herself. This time he wasn't going to get away with it. At the very least, he owed her an abject apology. After all, it was his damn job she was doing in the first place.

"Is that the truth, honey?" The husky appeal of Zackery's tone wrapped around Desiree's body like a warm blanket.

"Yes," she snapped, holding on to her righteous anger regardless of the temptation he offered.

"Thank you, Desiree," he whispered softly.

"For what?" she questioned, wary of his unexpected response.

"For taking on my problems, for giving up your weekend to finish those drawings. And for not hanging up on me while I made a fool out of myself by yelling at you like a demented maniac," he enumerated with careful precision.

In spite of herself, Desiree was unable to control the humor teasing at her with his last comment. Her lips quivered betrayingly at the accuracy of his final point. "You deserve it," she stated, only a slight tremor of amusement vibrating in the smooth slip of syllables.

The rumble of laughter in her ear echoed the grin spreading across her face. "I did, didn't I? Will you forgive me if I say I'm sorry?"

"Are you?" she shot back pertly.

"I am . . . very."

"Good," she announced, pleased and surprised to find her earlier mood returning. "Now can we start over from when I say hello?" Desiree was amazed at the flirtatious nature of her reply. Was this Desiree Beaumont speaking or some fantasy of her own creation?

"Hi, honey, did you miss me?"

Startled at the soft, provocative growl, Desiree

almost dropped the phone. "Yes . . . I mean, no."
She corrected herself hastily. Talk about creating a
fantasy! Zackery's deep greeting was all she could
have dreamed of and more. It carried the memory of
every moment they had shared and hinted at delights
yet unknown.

He chuckled at her stammered response. "I like
your first answer best so I'm ignoring the rest. Besides,
I missed you like the devil in spite of this mess we've
got here."

Not daring to believe the promise her ears seemed
to hear, she quelled the rising excitement growing
within her. She needed a diversion, any diversion.
Desiree gratefully seized on the reason for his trip.
"Was it as bad as you thought it would be?"

"Backtracking, Desiree?" Zackery gently mocked
her choice of subject.

"For the moment," she admitted. "Phones aren't
the most reliable method of communication, and we
do have a fairly large problem to handle."

"That should be my line," Zackery commented,
curiosity evident in spite of the distance separating
them. "Don't tell me I've spawned a monster by giving
you a little power."

Hitching her towel tighter around her breasts, Desiree curled up in the chair near her bed. "I'm not
really sure what you've done," she began slowly,
suddenly confronted with the change in her attitude.
She stared down at her bare legs tucked under her
where tiny beads of water still glistened on her tanned
skin. She had been so engrossed in her conversation,
she'd completely forgotten about how wet she was.

"Desiree?" The gentle prompting sought an explanation.

She sighed, vaguely irritated at his persistence in wanting to know something she barely understood herself.

"I'm not sure I can explain."

"Try," he urged.

"I feel responsible—not because I want to, I don't— but Dream Magic is mine. I won't see some sneaky thief ruin it with a lot of cheap, shoddy imitations."

"And you care?"

"Yes, damn it," she exploded, driven into an admission she didn't want to make. "Can it happen? Will it?"

Zackery sighed deeply. "I'm afraid it's a definite threat. The line was compromised. The police found the schedule of production, model stats and promo projections on our man when they picked him up."

"Blast!" Desiree swore vehemently. Then she brightened as the import of Zackery's words sank in. "If he still had it, he couldn't have passed it on."

"He could have made copies," he stated flatly.

Desiree's lips curved down in a disappointed frown. "I didn't consider that. Do you think he did?"

"I doubt it, but we don't dare count on it."

Desiree slumped in resignation. "I know. So it still means flat-out work for us." She paused, contemplating the prospect. "When are you coming back? Soon, I hope."

"At least a week," he answered shortly, frustration at the situation making his reply sharp. "Our little spy wasn't content with Dream Magic. Unfortunately he's been operating undetected for quite a while. Not only have I got to assess the scope of his activities, but the security around here is due for an overhaul. I won't have this happening again if I have to fire the whole department."

Sympathy for Zackery's problem welled up within her, as well as a surprising urge to smooth away the tension, anger and weariness she sensed in his voice. "You mean I'm keeping my power for a while?" she teased, hoping to lighten his mood.

"I'm counting on it," he growled.

The deep stroke of his affirmation brought a soft sparkle to Desiree's eyes. She pressed the receiver against her ear, needing the verbal warmth of Zackery as achingly as she longed for his touch.

How she loved this man. She was bewitched, lost in a passion so intense it seemed unreal. But it wasn't. This undeniable need was no figment of her imagination. It was vibrantly alive. Aware she had been daydreaming when she should have been paying attention, Desiree forced her mind back to the business at hand.

"What about the model for our image? Is she on her way? Or are we working from measurements?"

If Zackery was startled by Desiree's quick change of subject, it wasn't evident in his prompt reply. "She'll be on a plane first thing in the morning. I have to get back to work in a minute, but before I go, we'd better set up some kind of schedule between us to handle any unforeseen difficulties that may crop up." He paused a moment to give Desiree a chance to comment. When she didn't, he continued briskly. "I'll check in with you every evening about seven your time unless something urgent arises, then call me at the office. Marsha'll have the numbers. I trust your judgment, but I know with the rush we're having, you're being tossed into the deep end without a decent chance to get your toes wet. So if you need me, call."

Seconds later Desiree replaced the phone, a funny

little wistful yet sad smile tugging at her lips. Need him! God, what a laugh, she thought, glancing down at her hands. The fine tremor coursing through the slender bones was a mute testimony to the emotion spilling over the shattered barriers of her control.

One day, no, it wasn't even twenty-four hours until tomorrow morning. He'd been gone less than a day and here she was shaking with the physical pain of his absence. It was unlike anything she'd ever known. On top of that, she was committed to a business project she wasn't even sure she could handle even if she did have control of herself.

With a heartfelt groan, Desiree rose to her feet, restless, edgy, wanting to rush somewhere but knowing she could not. The confusion of her usually restrained responses was so out of character that for the moment she didn't know how to handle it. Her well-ordered life was shattered beyond recall. Zackery and Dream Magic filled her future, each bringing seemingly insurmountable problems. How was she to deal with either of them? For once in her life, there was no black or white answer. She was powerless to alter the coming days. She could and would devote her energies to breathing life into Dream Magic—but was that enough? Or would some slinking thief reap the benefits of her dreams? And Zackery? She had given him her body and her heart. She knew he desired the first, but did he want the last? Or was she only another of his women? She closed her eyes against the wrenching pain of the unpalatable thought. She wanted to believe in the wildfire attraction between them. Yet the past warned her too well against the blindness of faith.

Desiree tumbled into bed well after midnight, finally worn out by the unrelenting questions that wouldn't leave her in peace. There were no solutions, and she couldn't go back. She was committed heart and mind to the future.

Monday morning dawned all too soon, bringing with it the multitude of irritants designed to drive any sane person wild. It started mildly enough with a short staff meeting outlining the project before them and discussing the alterations each boss meant to employ to meet the demand.

Desiree was both pleased and relieved to note the acceptance she was accorded by her subordinates. She strongly suspected she had Marsha to thank for smoothing over the rough spots during her phoning the day before. When Desiree left the conference room with the new production workup in her hand, she felt more confident about Dream Magic's introduction to the fashion world.

She should have known better. The first problem to darken her horizon was the absence of their Dream Magic girl aboard her plane. Several calls, each more provoking than the last, found her still in New York finishing up her previous assignment. Stifling her anger at the mixup, Desiree took down the model's measurements and got them off to the pattern people. Then there were the jewelry accessories to choose for Temptress as well as for the four new designs from Sunday, meetings with the ad people to discuss the feasibility of various approaches to promotion which would garner the immediate coverage they needed and so on it went. . . . By seven, Desiree was certain nothing good was going to come out of the chaos on her desk.

She slumped back in her seat, glaring at the endless lists in front of her, the most important one being the proposal for the launching of Dream Magic at an exclusive showing in one of the major hotels. Marsha had done an excellent job of getting the agenda prepared for her approval in such a short time. So much so, Desiree felt honor bound to get it back to her equally fast so she could finalize the arrangements. She fingered the precisely compiled report, her gaze fastened on the date of the show, the tenth. Nine days! She shook her head at the time left. One day for every gown still uncompleted!

The ring of the phone at her elbow shattered the silence of her office. Desiree reached for the receiver, her mind still caught up in the papers she had been studying.

"What the devil are you doing at the office? You should have been home an hour ago." Zackery rumbled ominously. "Do you have any idea what time it is?"

"Yes," she snapped, her frayed temper reacting immediately to the irritated demand in his voice. "And if you're going to yell at me again, I warn you right now I'm in no mood for it." Almost hoping he would ignore her warning, Desiree's eyes gleamed molten jade with angry anticipation. Frustration had dogged her footsteps all afternoon and she was itching to let fly. Zackery made such a perfect target.

"That bad, huh?" Zackery murmured on a quieter note. "Want to tell me about it? I might be able to help."

The understanding and sympathy of his warm reply defused Desiree's annoyance. "The only way you can help is to get on the first plane home. Failing that, you could create about eight more days to add to the time between now and next Tuesday," she suggested wryly.

"Why don't you give me a rundown on what's been

happening. I know Stella messed up the schedule by missing the plane. Is that all of it or is there more?"

Feeling immeasurably better by the moment, Desiree sighed and relaxed her tense muscles. Just hearing Zackery was almost as reassuring as having him beside her, she realized with sudden perception.

"Most of it's minor stuff," she explained finally. "I think I'm just panicking for no reason."

His denial was satisfyingly prompt. "Believe me, honey, you're doing fine."

"How do you know?" she demanded, curious about the certainty in his tone.

"I know you, remember? I keep telling you, you can handle this. In fact, you might even find you enjoy it."

Desiree leaned her head back against the chair, her eyes half closed as she considered his words. "In a way, you're right," she began slowly, a faint hint of surprise betraying the shock of her discovery. "It is satisfying to work out a problem and see it through to its conclusion. Like revamping this development schedule, choosing the jewelry and accessories to go with the mood of my gowns . . . even the preparations for the show are going well. Although the credit for that goes to Marsha. All I have to do is okay the arrangements."

"It sounds like you've got a good start," Zackery complimented her.

"A start, yes," she agreed without hesitation. "But it's the finish that counts."

"I know, but you did well today, so there's no reason to assume you won't do as well tomorrow."

Somehow Zackery's unstinting support in the face of her continued anxiety made Desiree feel about two years old. He was right, she acknowledged silently.

She had done fine until now. The panic she was feeling was nothing more than a reaction to the sudden shift in the way of life she had always known. But that didn't mean she was incapable. It only meant she was inexperienced. She had a good mind, a sharp sense of business in spite of her efforts to deny it, and she knew Dream Magic better than anyone. She could handle it. Suddenly Desiree felt her worries and fears fall away. Zackery believed in her and, as Marsha so eloquently put it, where business was concerned, Zackery was completely impersonal. With that kind of faith behind her, Desiree felt a traitor if she did not trust herself.

"Thank you," she whispered softly, aware of the gift he had given her. "I don't think I'll ever want to be in this position again, but I'm truly glad I'm here now. I think I've been needing a situation like this for a long time, but until you made me face it, I've never had the courage to tackle it. I'm beginning to understand myself and to see things I've never known before."

"I wish I were home," Zackery groaned deeply. "I miss you, little cat. These two days have seemed like years."

Responding to the rich sound curling about her body, Desiree nestled into her chair in an unconscious effort to create the illusion of Zackery's arms cradling her. "I wish it were over."

"That makes two of us. Whether or not I get things finished up here, I'll come back for the show."

"Those nine days are destined to haunt me," Desiree purred feelingly. The desire unfurling within her lent a forlorn note to her voice.

"Hell . . ." Zackery swore violently. "This telephoning is no damn good at all. I want to hold you in my arms, kiss every golden inch of you, make love to you—and I can't even see your face. I need the feel of you next to me when I sleep. This verbal lovemaking is killing me . . . us." He ended on a deep groan of male desire a second before continuing in a startlingly brisk tone. "Listen, honey cat, I'm coming back tonight. Hang up so I can get a flight."

Shaken by the seductive quality of his words, Desiree took a moment to react to his abrupt change of mood. When the sense of what he said hit her, she sat bolt upright in shock. "No, Zackery, you can't," she gasped, the absolute decision in his voice dispelling her passionate imagery as nothing else could have done. "You've got to stay there. There's too much at stake to come hurrying back here and I've got too much going to give it up."

She felt him hesitate as though considering her request. "Please stay there, do what you must. Let me prove myself . . . to me," she pleaded, then added, "I'll be waiting for you when we're both free."

"Is that a promise?" he questioned quickly. "You'll stay with me, be my woman, my lover?"

Desiree gripped the receiver tightly, knowing the commitment he demanded. She reminded herself that he wasn't speaking of love, but her heart ignored her inner voice. Her love was strong enough for two. She would hide no longer. He wanted her—his very words conveyed his need and his desire—she would take what he offered.

"Yes, I'll be here when you come home."

"Soon as I can, my own," Zackery drawled in a deep throb of possession before gently replacing the receiver.

Desiree held the softly buzzing instrument in her hands, her fingers curved lovingly around the smooth contours. Her senses remembered the velvet brush of

Zackery's flesh beneath her palms as he lay in her arms.

"I love you," she whispered in the silence. "I love you." With a sigh of contentment, she hung up the phone, placed the papers on her desk into a locked drawer and collected her handbag. It was time to go home.

In the days that followed, Desiree found herself assuming more responsibility and gaining confidence in her own judgment. She still had little liking for the marketplace and its frenzied pace, but she was learning to understand it. For Desiree, this change in attitude had begun with Zackery, but it had taken the demands of Dream Magic on Z.T.'s staff to crystalize her altered viewpoint. Her biased judgments, based on her parents' extremist views, fell by the wayside while respect and, in some cases, admiration blossomed for the people of the Taylor/Maxwell organization as they pushed themselves to fulfill the needs of the new line. Everyone from the office messengers to the highest level of management seemed bent on attaining one goal—presenting her fantasy to the public.

And Zackery. His nightly calls were a source of encouragement and a fountain of knowledge Desiree drew from unreservedly. His business acumen coupled with her creative flair should have been at odds, yet strangely they were uniquely compatible. The wedding of their personalities strengthened the bond between them, creating a new dimension of emotion on Desiree's side, if not Zackery's. The feelings she had for her dark-eyed lover increased daily, and the ache she felt grew more intense with each passing moment of his absence.

By Monday afternoon, twenty-four hours before

the big show, Desiree was exhausted both mentally and physically, and literally counting the seconds until Zackery's arrival. He had promised faithfully to be home in time for the preview on Tuesday.

"Desiree?"

The soft-voiced query drew Desiree's attention from the order of the lingerie presentation she had been working on. She glanced up to see Mary Beth hovering in her doorway. Desiree smiled gently at her eager young secretary.

"Yes?" she prompted, a delicate brow arched questioningly at the interruption.

"Ms. James is on her way up with the final tally of acceptances for tomorrow. Shall I make some coffee for you both and maybe a sandwich?"

The mention of food made Desiree check her watch. A flicker of surprise crossed her face before she shook her head at her own forgetfulness. "I did it again, didn't I?" she murmured. "That's the third time I've forgotten to eat lunch."

"Fourth, but who's counting?" Marsha corrected breezily. She brushed past Mary Beth's petite form with a quick apology. "How about ordering us a chicken salad each and a chocolate shake. I'm starving," she added, plopping herself down on the edge of Desiree's desk and grinning unashamedly.

"Okay, sergeant," Desiree chuckled. "Make it three, Mary Beth. I know you didn't go out either." She frowned slightly as she watched her secretary return to her office. "Thank heaven this will all be over by tomorrow night. There were times when I didn't think we'd make it."

"Amen," Marsha agreed with a heartfelt groan. "Come Wednesday I'm putting in for a week's rest just to recuperate."

Desiree gazed at her visitor, her expression conveying her disbelief. "Sure you are." She held out her hand for the sheath of papers the other woman held. "Give me those things and quit telling lies. You know you've loved every minute of this crazy week."

Marsha shrugged gracefully, not bothering to deny the truth of Desiree's statement. "Well, for somebody who's really more comfortable sketching, you did a pretty good job yourself. Even the boss says so."

Startled at the mention of Zackery, Desiree looked up quickly, a question in her golden green gaze. "Did you talk to him today?"

Marsha nodded. "A while ago. He said to tell you not to expect to hear from him tonight and that he'd see you tomorrow afternoon."

The lovely anticipation of his evening call died abruptly. Desiree could only stare at her wordlessly. She read the knowledge of her love for Zackery in Marsha's eyes, and she was surprised at the lack of disapproval or censure. True, there was a disturbing glint in the usually cool depths, as though Marsha knew something she didn't, but that was all.

"Anything else?" Desiree prompted, having the oddest feeling that whatever information Marsha had was somehow important to her.

Marsha shook her glossy head, the faint gleam becoming a decided twinkle. "Not a thing." She hesitated for a split second.

Desiree leaned forward slightly, her breath catching in her throat.

"He did say to tell you he was sorry he didn't call you himself, but he had to get to a meeting."

Disappointed, Desiree leaned back in her chair with a sigh. "At least he's going to be here for the show," she offered, hoping to cover her disappointment.

"I'm sure he will be," Marsha observed with suspicious blandness. She flicked a slender red-tipped finger against the list Desiree held. "What do you think of our guests?"

The abrupt change of subject was typical of the secretary and a trait which Desiree had come to accept without question. "Very impressive. Much better than I would have thought we'd have on such short notice."

Marsha opened her lips to reply but was forestalled by the reappearance of Mary Beth bearing their late lunch.

"Z.T. better appreciate the sacrifices we're making," Marsha announced, sliding agilely off the desk. She wasted no time in taking her place on one end of the couch.

Desiree sat down on the other and gestured for Mary Beth to take the remaining chair.

"I'm sure Mr. Maxwell knows how hard you've worked," Mary Beth offered shyly, her glance divided equally between the two older women.

Desiree and Marsha exchanged a look of rueful understanding. Oh, to be young again and gazing at the world with all the open-handed trust of untarnished ideals.

"Well, if he doesn't I'll be sure to remind him when I see him Tuesday," Marsha murmured outrageously between bites of chicken salad. "We females have to stand up for our rights nowadays." She grinned conspiratorially at Desiree.

Desiree raised her styrofoam cup in salute. "I'll drink to that," she intoned solemnly before breaking into husky laughter at the thought of having to enforce her rights with Zackery.

He was the man who treated her as a person in her

own right and as an equal. Whether he loved her or not, that one fact stood out in their relationship. Warmed by his very clear regard, Desiree knew a feeling of immeasurable security unlike anything she had ever experienced. Whatever the future held for her and Zackery, she knew she would never regret her time in Houston and the part of her that she had shared with this very special man. His influence in her life had finally laid to rest the ghosts of the past. She was no longer the woman who had to hide behind a mask to protect herself. She was finally free to accept the person she was. In a very real way, her fantasy had come to life.

For that Zackery was responsible.

10

It was late evening by the time Desiree unlocked her apartment and padded wearily toward her bedroom. She had stayed over purposely to shorten the long hours stretching before her without Zackery's nightly call. Tonight should have been a celebration of their efforts, she thought disappointedly, although a long-distance one. They had made it! All that was left was the preview itself.

Desiree knew the satisfaction she felt was a pale imitation of the elation she would have shared with Zackery. He had become so much a part of her life and her thoughts, the absence of his phone call made their achievements seem curiously flat. Shaking her head over her unusual dependence on another person, Desiree slipped out of her clothes and tumbled into bed. For once she had no desire to bother with a nightgown. All she wanted now was the sweet oblivion of dreamland to rest her aching body and her lonely heart. Sleep claimed her almost immediately.

A thundering insistent pounding accompanied by impatient buzzes pierced Desiree's slumber. Groggy, more asleep than awake, she raised her tousled head and frowned in the darkness. The thuds continued with unabated power, punctuated by a decidedly sharp peal of her doorbell.

Lifting a bare arm to brush the tangled fall of curls from her half-opened eyes, Desiree scrambled awkwardly from the covers. Sheer reflex made her step into the cobalt silk, thigh-length kimono she usually draped on a chair near her bed at night.

She tied the thin sash as she stumbled her way through her darkened unfamiliar apartment to the door.

"I'm coming," she muttered irritably as her bare feet hit the cool stone floor of the entranceway.

"Desiree?"

The deep questioning voice easily penetrated the thickness of the door.

"Zackery?" Desiree echoed, the veils of her disturbed sleep dispelled at the knowledge of Zackery's presence on her doorstep.

"Let me in, honey," he commanded.

Her usual graceful, coordinated movements conspicuously absent, Desiree fumbled with the chain. Mumbling a few choice epithets in a not-so-quiet voice, she finally succeeded in releasing the lock. Zackery's soft masculine chuckle coincided precisely with her opening the door.

A thousand and one emotions filtered through Desiree's mind as she stood blinking at her unheralded but most anxiously awaited visitor, each more demanding, more potent than the last. Surprise, happiness, joy, excitement and finally, just plain need. The sight of his lean, angled face and the velvet-brown caress of his eyes called to the lonely ache in her being, filling it, soothing away the pain of his absence.

"Zackery." The husky drawl of his name carried every nuance of her feelings. She stood poised and waiting, silhouetted in the inky shadows of her apartment.

"Desiree," Zackery murmured huskily, stepping forward the one pace needed to bring him within a heartbeat of her still figure. His smoldering gaze roamed across her sleep-flushed face as though he had never seen her before.

The heat of his glance seared Desiree's skin, drawing her nearer. His arms closed around her pliant body, carefully, gently enfolding her against the rock-hard planes of his frame. A long, shuddering sigh rippled the mass of disheveled ash brown curls as Desiree's cheek came to rest naturally against the warmth of his chest. The scent of his cologne mingled with the rich aroma that was pure Zackery, creating a wine-potent spell of desire.

"Never again," Zackery vowed in a roughened rasp. "When I leave the next time, you're coming with me."

Desiree raised her head to stare into rich pools of banked male hunger. "I am?" she whispered.

He nodded, his face cast in a ruthless mold Desiree recognized as unrelenting determination. "You're my woman. Where I go, you go." He bent his head, capturing her lips in a kiss that conveyed the full range of his emotions, the need, the desire, the gentleness and the strength. But most of all, he told her of his love. Perhaps unknowingly, yet it was silently there—clear, vibrant, glowingly alive. It was all Desiree hoped; it was what she needed more than air to breathe and she accepted it with a lover's greed, returning it full measure.

Somewhere in the exchange of unspoken commitment, a door thudded shut and the darkness of her home became a world of sensory delight—the crisp feel of Zackery's hair beneath her fingers; the sweet, intoxicating taste of his mouth surrounding hers; the warm moisture of his cat-rough tongue as it searched out the hidden secrets of her own mouth.

"God, woman, it's been much too long," he whispered hoarsely when he freed her lips to draw in a deep breath. With a sweep of his body, he lifted her high into his arms and strode confidently through the darkness to her bedroom.

Here the black shadows were washed with silver from the full moon outside the open windows. The iridescent glow played gently over Desiree's soft silk-covered curves and the sharper planes and angles of Zackery's face as he lowered her carefully onto the sheets.

His dark eyes traced the slender lines of Desiree's length, a tiny twist of his lips revealing his appreciation of the barely adequate kimono. He reached for the sash and deftly untied the single knot at her waist. His gaze caressed her face as his fingers drifted over her robe to reveal the golden skin it enfolded.

Caught in the throbbing intimacy of his visual hold, Desiree touched the tip of her tongue to tingling lips.

"I know." He groaned, his eyes lingering on the betraying movement. He began to remove his coat. "I want you just as much. I don't think my body has stopped aching for you since the moment I left."

Desiree was aware of a fine quiver running through him as he stood only inches away. He fumbled slightly in his haste to undo the buttons on his cuffs. She smiled tenderly at the small indications of his arousal. "Me, too," she breathed. "In the day it wasn't so bad, but the nights . . . ! My dreams were never so real or so unfulfilling."

"I'm glad," he admitted with the supreme satisfaction of a man who had claimed his woman. He came down on the bed beside her to gather her into his arms. "I want to own you, every thought, every emotion, every inch of your beautiful body. But I want you to be free in every way to be the passionate woman you are. I want you to come to me, live with me and love me."

Stunned by the all-consuming depth of Zackery's commitment, Desiree had no words to give him. Instead she drew him into her softness, opening her lips to the sweet ravishment of his mouth.

She moaned deep in her throat at the surrender of her body to the hardness of his. He moved over her in a tantalizing claim of possession, touching, caressing, sensitizing every inch of her from the tiny nerve behind her ear to the special spot of exotic sensation at her ankle.

Loving him, wanting desperately to know his full power, Desiree arched into his touch. She curved her hands around the firm flesh at his waist, demandingly.

"Zackery, I need you. . . ." She gasped, the blazing heat of his passion burning within her.

"Slowly, woman," he soothed, sliding his fingers intimately along the inner softness of her leg. "We have all night."

Desiree buried one hand on the thickness of the hair on his chest and tugged in blatant warning. "I want you *now*." She growled her feminine demand for the satisfaction only he could give.

Zackery responded as though her cry was the signal he had been waiting for. With a gesture of strength and masculine beauty, he moved above her, his knee slipping naturally between her thighs to make room for his entry.

"Oh Zackery." His name was torn from the very depths of Desiree's being as Zackery completed their union in one graceful fluid drive to the secret inner core of her femininity.

Desiree's fingers clenched the rippling muscles of Zackery's shoulders and back, then reached down to tighten violently around his hips.

Lost in a world of taste, touch and feel, Desiree clung to the source and haven of the desire sending quivers of need rushing through her limbs. She surrendered her body to the magical rhythm Zackery created for their pleasure. Lips met lips, fusing in an ultimate wish for oneness, creating a searing, blazing trail stretching to the farthest reaches of human experience. Faster, higher, hurry now . . . we're almost . . .

Twin cries of the final fierce claiming echoed across the continuum of the lovers' universe. Equal in power, unique to each, a bond was forged to unite this man and this woman.

Then peace . . . the gentle, waiting rest of complete fulfillment washed across their heated bodies like waves against a thirsty shore. In the moonlit room, Desiree lay in Zackery's secure embrace, her face snug against his chest, his arms locking her against his love-dampened body.

Unable to resist the temptation of the moist scent tantalizing her senses, Desiree flicked out the tip of her tongue to whimsically trace a "D" across his chest.

Rousing at the delicate touch, Zackery stretched lazily. "It was almost worth the wait," he whispered teasingly.

"You think so, do you?" Desiree wriggled enticingly, enjoying the male weight of him crushing her body into the mattress.

"Umm," he agreed, his chin against her hair. He eased onto his side while still managing to keep Desiree trapped beside him.

"I had a feeling those drawings of yours were something special. There was a sensuality about them that intrigued me."

"Personally, I thought of them as erotic," Desiree mumbled, only half listening. The feel of Zackery's body was much too intoxicating a subject not to investigate. Long, tapering fingers began a slow, provocative search of Zackery's replete form, starting with the broad expanse of furred chest.

Zackery's hiss of indrawn breath told her of his susceptibility. "That, too," he rumbled near her ear. He arched into her questing fingers, obviously enjoying her exploration. "If you keep on doing that, you're not going to hear how long I've been waiting for you."

"I'm listening," Desiree taunted wickedly, her golden green eyes alight with mischief and smoldering desire.

Zackery's large hand captured Desiree's adventurous smaller one, holding it pressed to his chest just over his heart. "I mean it, honey. I think we ought to talk."

Desiree lifted her head and stared into his soft velvet eyes, seeing the determination there. "I thought we had," she whispered at last, puzzled by the urgency in his voice.

"Not about this," he denied. "I've wanted to often enough, but I kept putting it off." He grinned ruefully, his gaze warmly caressing her bewildered features. "It's tough for a man of my age and so-called experience to admit to a fantasy."

"A fantasy?" Desiree echoed, completely lost. "What fantasy?"

Zackery's dark brows rose in pretended offense at her confused reaction.

"Zackery," Desiree prompted.

He relented with a soft chuckle. "My love, I've been dying to get you just where you are from the moment I finished looking at those sketches of yours."

Barely hearing the rest of his statement, Desiree focused on his first two words. "Your what?" she breathed.

"My love," he repeated on a deepening note. He released her hand to curve his fingers around her throat. He stared deep into her love-softened gaze, all traces of teasing wiped from his face. "I love you, Desiree. I think I have almost from the first moment you came gliding into my office. I love everything about you from the top of your delightfully abandoned curls to the soles of your slender feet."

"You do?" Desiree searched his serious features, needing to see the truth his voice told her.

He nodded. "It seems like I've loved you forever, yet I know we haven't known each other long. But time doesn't matter. I won't let it." He tightened his hold on her slender curves as though trying to draw her into himself.

Desiree raised a hand to his bronzed cheek, her fingers rubbing lightly over the stubble of his beard. "I love you, Zackery Taylor Maxwell," she assured him, the strength of her commitment making her voice a rich cadence of sound in the silence of their loving place.

"Enough to put away your solitude and stay with me?" Zackery pressed his forefinger to her lips before she could answer. "I meant what I said. I want all of you, just as I'll give you all of me. There'll be no other for either of us."

Desiree gently kissed the finger pressed to her lips. He lifted it. "There never has been anyone else who mattered. Only you."

"You're certain?"

She nodded, feeling the tension in his body drain away with a deep sigh. "I'm sure. I have been since the day after you left."

"Good, then that marriage license I got for us will be worth everything I did to get it," he murmured complacently. Tucking her body close to his, he settled himself comfortably for sleep.

"Marriage?" Desiree squeaked, lifting her head off his shoulder with a jerk.

One hand slipped around her nape and guided it back into place. "After the show tomorrow night, you and I are going to have a nice long honeymoon. We earned it."

In spite of her confusion, Desiree couldn't resist the warmth of the body stretched against hers. Nuzzling into his firm contours, she breathed a soft sigh. "But should we get married? What about my job . . . the Dream Magic promotion—"

"Hush," Zackery commanded, interrupting her list of complications. "One, you can work or not as you choose. Two, Jim and Marsha are perfectly well equipped to handle whatever crops up now—you did a damn nice job getting it into production, but we both know you'd much prefer to go back to your drawing board. And finally, I love you and you love me so why the devil should we wait around for days to make it legal?"

Why indeed? Desiree wondered on a smothered giggle. "Is this a sample of your businessman's logic?" she asked interestedly.

"No," Zackery denied immediately. "It's called desperation for you." He readjusted himself more comfortably against the pillows. "I don't suppose we could continue this discussion in the morning. I'm beat and we do have a busy day waiting for us."

Amusement at his plaintive tone vied with irritation at his assumption that she would marry him. "We're *not* going to sleep until we get this straightened out," Desiree decreed.

"I thought we were straight," Zackery murmured drowsily, his breath a warm fan of air across her cheek.

Desiree gave her lazy mate an ungentle poke in the ribs. "In a pig's eye," she retorted indignantly. "You haven't asked me to marry you at all. You've just spelled out the situation like some damn merger. If this is a sample of what being married to you holds in store for the future, then I decline the honor."

Zackery opened his eyes to stare down into Desiree's rebellious face. For a moment, he contemplated her without speaking.

Desiree glared back at him. She might love this man to distraction, but she wasn't stupid enough to allow him to set the rules without even discussing them with her first.

"Well, I suppose if you're really set on it, we could

just live together." One dark brow quirked interrogatingly as he waited for her reaction. "Although why you'd want such a thing is beyond me," he continued, suspiciously bland.

"Zackery Maxwell," Desiree gritted, pushing at the arm that held her chained to his side.

"Desiree Beaumont," Zackery mimicked, ignoring her bid for freedom. His free hand lifted her chin so he could see her stormy eyes. "Please marry me, my love," he whispered huskily. "Come live with me and share my life."

The softly spoken question stilled Desiree's struggle, the fight in her draining away as though it had never been. Her golden green gaze searched his face. Reassured by the love and understanding she saw mirrored there, she relaxed against Zackery once more. "Yes," she answered on a breathy sigh. "But don't think you're always going to get around me this easily," she warned on a firmer note.

Zackery grinned slowly, his lips twisting at her independence. He bent his head until his mouth hovered a breath away from hers. "Never," he affirmed unhesitatingly. "I've got too much respect for your strength and your spirit. As well as a high regard for my personal safety."

The outrageous comment tickled Desiree's sense of humor. A chuckle escaped as her eyes gleamed with appreciation. "Now we may sleep," she commanded with regal hauteur, joining in his half-teasing banter.

Her molten jade eyes locked with brown velvet in deep communication beyond their light words. The hand holding her chin gently slipped down her throat to capture the life-throbbing pulse in its vulnerable hollow. Desiree's fingers traced delicately over his jaw before outlining the firm contours of his lips with one forefinger. Desire, still smoldering, leapt to life between them.

"Are you very tired?" Desiree purred, the tip of her tongue tracking the edge of her lips in a sensuous imitation of her tracing of Zackery's mouth.

He shook his head, his eyes intent on her provocative gesture. "I think I'm being manipulated," he rasped as he drew her toward him.

"Don't you like it?" Desiree flowed over Zackery's body, melting against him.

"I love it," he growled just before his lips captured hers in a hungry, pleading, demanding kiss conveying the full spectrum of his love for his woman. A demand Desiree met with equal power as she lay claim to her love, her man.

Forever after, Desiree remembered the Dream Magic presentation with a sense of pride and awe at the response her fantasy created. From the moment she and Zackery arrived at the hotel to supervise the behind-the-scenes, last-minute details and greet the guests, everything went like clockwork. The last-second appearance of Laura, the instigator of Desiree's finally stepping out on her own, was an added bonus. And when Laura made no effort to hide her blatant I-told-you-so smile or her obvious satisfaction at the relationship between her and Zackery, Desiree was unable to summon the smallest desire to pop her friend's bubble of pleased self-importance. Instead, smiling, she hurried Laura into one of the seats in the front row saved for her and Zackery.

Zackery materialized at her side just long enough to greet the sparkling blonde before whisking Desiree backstage to a vantage point where they could view the show.

Sweet Surrender led the parade of Desiree's designs before the formal gathering of the fashion world's elite. A vision of frothy white chiffon and delicate silver threads, it was designed to portray the virginal innocence of a woman's first love. Vision after vision flowed across the raised platform to the strains of individually selected background music. The silence from the appreciative audience was total and a perfect accolade to Desiree's unique style and flair.

But the highlight of the gala was Golden Temptress. Lights dimmed in preparation for its entrance. Then, in a swell of primitive jungle rhythm, Marla, the lynx-eyed Eurasian model Desiree had chosen to display her favorite dream, undulated into view. A concerted "Ahh" of stunned attention greeted her spectacular appearance. Spotlights caught the gold-shot silk showering the spellbound audience with gilt tracings. The basic style of the one-shoulder slither of fabric was stunningly simple, relying on the cunning cut of the gown to mold to the wearer's form like a lover's embrace. The waist-high side slit in the skirt dared every male eye in the room to guess what was holding the pulsating wisp in place.

"That is not going out on the open market," Zackery growled against Desiree's ear.

Desiree leaned back against his chest, enjoying her moment of triumph as the applause of her guests carried backstage. Her dream was a smashing success —just as Zackery had told her it would be.

"Do I detect a note of territorial instinct in that?" she teased, almost purring as Zackery's hands slid intimately down the amber silk of her wrap gown.

"Mmm," he murmured huskily, nuzzling her neck. "You do, witch. The only woman I know who could ever do justice to that gown is you, my love."

"Ms. Beaumont."

The excited summons broke the small world of sensuous awareness, jolting Desiree back to the present.

"They want you on stage."

Slowly, with obvious reluctance, Zackery released Desiree. He smiled wickedly down at her as she hesitated, clearly torn between staying with him or greeting the crowd that was going wild out front.

"Go on, woman. Take your bows so we can get to that honeymoon." He prodded her with a devilish gleam in his eye.

Desiree met his provocative comment with a challenge of her own. Lowering her lashes, she gave him her best cat stare. Then swaying ever so gently, she recreated Marla's seductive stroll. Only hers was the real thing, no pale imitation to show off a beautiful gown. Hips flowing into a stride of pure pagan witchery, she glided away, leaving him aware of every glorious, talented curve of her sensuous body.

"Don't forget to have the wardrobe mistress box Temptress for you," she purred just before she disappeared in front of the stage curtain.

Zackery's eyes were glued to the spot she had left. "On second thought, who the devil needs it? I have the original." He groaned deeply, savoring the knowledge of the delights awaiting him in the years to come.

Silhouette Desire
15-Day Trial Offer

A new romance series
that explores
contemporary relationships
in exciting detail

Six Silhouette Desire romances, free for 15 days!
We'll send you six new Silhouette Desire romances
to look over for 15 days, absolutely free! If you decide
not to keep the books, return them and owe nothing.

Six books a month, free home delivery. If you like
Silhouette Desire romances as much as we think you
will, keep them and return your payment with the
invoice. Then we will send you six new books every
month to preview, just as soon as they are published.
You pay only for the books you decide to keep, and
you never pay postage and handling.

YOU'LL BE SWEPT AWAY WITH SILHOUETTE DESIRE

$1.75 each

1 ☐ James

2 ☐ Monet

3 ☐ Clay

4 ☐ Carey

5 ☐ Baker

6 ☐ Mallory

7 ☐ St. Claire

8 ☐ Dee

9 ☐ Simms

10 ☐ Smith

$1.95 each

11 ☐ James

12 ☐ Palmer

13 ☐ Wallace

14 ☐ Valley

15 ☐ Vernon

16 ☐ Major

17 ☐ Simms

18 ☐ Ross

19 ☐ James

20 ☐ Allison

21 ☐ Baker

22 ☐ Durant

23 ☐ Sunshine

24 ☐ Baxter

25 ☐ James

26 ☐ Palmer

27 ☐ Conrad

28 ☐ Lovan

29 ☐ Michelle

30 ☐ Lind

31 ☐ James

32 ☐ Clay

33 ☐ Powers

34 ☐ Milan

35 ☐ Major

36 ☐ Summers

37 ☐ James

38 ☐ Douglass

39 ☐ Monet

40 ☐ Mallory

41 ☐ St. Claire

42 ☐ Stewart

43 ☐ Simms

44 ☐ West

45 ☐ Clay

46 ☐ Chance

47 ☐ Michelle

48 ☐ Powers

49 ☐ James

50 ☐ Palmer

51 ☐ Lind

52 ☐ Morgan

53 ☐ Joyce

54 ☐ Fulford

55 ☐ James

56 ☐ Douglass

57 ☐ Michelle

58 ☐ Mallory

59 ☐ Powers

60 ☐ Dennis

61 ☐ Simms

62 ☐ Monet

63 ☐ Dee

64 ☐ Milan

65 ☐ Allison

66 ☐ Langtry

67 ☐ James

68 ☐ Browning

69 ☐ Carey

70 ☐ Victor

71 ☐ Joyce

72 ☐ Hart

73 ☐ St. Clair

74 ☐ Douglass

75 ☐ McKenna

76 ☐ Michelle

77 ☐ Lowell

78 ☐ Barber

79 ☐ Simms

80 ☐ Palmer

81 ☐ Kennedy

82 ☐ Clay

YOU'LL BE SWEPT AWAY WITH SILHOUETTE DESIRE

$1.95 each

83 ☐ Chance	90 ☐ Roszel	97 ☐ James	104 ☐ Chase
84 ☐ Powers	91 ☐ Browning	98 ☐ Joyce	105 ☐ Blair
85 ☐ James	92 ☐ Carey	99 ☐ Major	106 ☐ Michelle
86 ☐ Malek	93 ☐ Berk	100 ☐ Howard	107 ☐ Chance
87 ☐ Michelle	94 ☐ Robbins	101 ☐ Morgan	108 ☐ Gladstone
88 ☐ Trevor	95 ☐ Summers	102 ☐ Palmer	
89 ☐ Ross	96 ☐ Milan	103 ☐ James	

SILHOUETTE DESIRE, Department SD/6
1230 Avenue of the Americas
New York, NY 10020

Please send me the books I have checked above. I am enclosing $_____
(please add 75¢ to cover postage and handling. NYS and NYC residents please
add appropriate sales tax). Send check or money order—no cash or C.O.D.'s
please. Allow six weeks for delivery.

NAME_____

ADDRESS_____

CITY_____ STATE/ZIP_____

Love, passion and adventure will be yours FREE for 15 days... with Tapestry™ historical romances!

"Long before women could read and write, tapestries were used to record events and stories . . . especially the exploits of courageous knights and their ladies."

And now there's a new kind of tapestry...

In the pages of Tapestry™ romance novels, you'll find love, intrigue, and historical touches that really make the stories come alive!

You'll meet brave Guyon d'Arcy, a Norman knight . . . handsome Comte Andre de Crillon, a Huguenot royalist . . . rugged Branch Taggart, a feuding American rancher . . . and more. And on each journey back in time, you'll experience tender romance and searing passion . . . and learn about the way people lived and loved in earlier times than ours.

We think you'll be so delighted with Tapestry romances, you won't want to miss a single one! We'd like to send you 2 books each month, as soon as they are published, through our Tapestry Home Subscription Service℠ Look them over for 15 days, free. If not delighted, simply return them and owe nothing. But if you enjoy them as much as we think you will, pay the invoice enclosed. There's never any additional charge for this convenient service — we pay all postage and handling costs.

To receive your Tapestry historical romances, fill out the coupon below and mail it to us today. You're on your way to all the love, passion, and adventure of times gone by!

HISTORICAL *Tapestry* ROMANCES

Tapestry™ is a trademark of Simon & Schuster.

READERS' COMMENTS ON SILHOUETTE DESIRES

"Thank you for Silhouette Desires. They are the best thing that has happened to the bookshelves in a long time."
—V.W.*, Knoxville, TN

"Silhouette Desires—wonderful, fantastic—the best romance around."
—H.T.*, Margate, N.J.

"As a writer as well as a reader of romantic fiction, I found DESIREs most refreshingly realistic—and definitely as magical as the love captured on their pages."
—C.M.*, Silver Lake, N.Y.

*names available on request